The
Misadventures
of
Rosie Petunia

Cristina Salgado Glasnovich

Nick Glasnovich

The Misadventures of Rosie Petunia

Published by: Dogs of Truth, LLC
Weehawken, New Jersey 07086
Info@DogsofTruth.com

First Hardcover & Paperback Editions
February 2021
ISBN 978-1-7365232-1-6 (Paperback)
ISBN 978-1-7365232-4-7 (Hardcover)

"Magic is believing in yourself,
if you can do that, you can
make anything happen."

- Johann Wolfgang von Goethe

CONTENTS

THANK YOU!

Thank you to all of those who helped make this book possible. Without your support, Rosie would just be a forgotten file buried deep on some hard drive.

THANK YOU...

Adam

Amanda

Andrea

Arthur

Dan & Sloane

Dorothy

Fernando & Maria

Joe & Lyndsey

Jordan

Lindsey

Mary Kay

Quincy

Sienna

Tom & Vicki

Victoria

Prologue

The Very, Very Beginning...

The first drop of rain hit Lux right on the top of her head, matting down her bright blonde hair. It was a big rain drop; the kind you get from a sudden, late spring thunderstorm. The drop was cold, too. Much colder than it should have been for this time of year.

Lux shivered as the icy water ran down her back. Without a word, she and her twin sister, Scura, ran for the cover of a nearby willow tree. They had been gathering wild blackberries in the middle of a

1

forest clearing near their home when the rain started.

The storm came out of nowhere. Moments before the first drops fell, the bright blue day suddenly filled with dark, angry clouds. Flashes of lightning spread across the sky, making the gloomy horizon look like a dark gray vase covered in brilliant white cracks. Booms of thunder shook the air.

Somehow, the sisters knew this wasn't going to be a quick spring storm; so, they ran as fast as they could down the wooded trail back toward home.

Not even halfway down the trail, the storm had grown more intense than either of the girls had ever seen. They could barely see through the pelting rain.

"Scura! A cave!" Lux shouted over the wind pointing to a dark gap in the mountainside.

Without a word, Scura sprinted as fast as she could toward the cavern. Lux was right on her heels.

Out of breath, completely soaked and giggling hysterically, Lux and Scura burst through the opening of the cave. Inside the cave was dark as night, but at least it was dry.

Scura was the first to catch her breath. Smoothing back her wavy, dark purple hair, she looked around and said, "I've never seen a storm like this come out of nowhere before."

Lux replied, "Yeah, but at least we found this cave."

Looking around at their new surroundings, Lux continued, "We've been picking berries in that field for years. Why have we never noticed this cave before today?"

"I don't know," Scura said, "But, I'm really glad it's here! Plus," she gave the basket of berries a little shake, "at least we have a snack."

With that, Scura and Lux settled in to enjoy their blackberries, watch the storm and wait for the rain to stop.

The two sisters must have fallen asleep, because the next thing Scura knew, the rain had stopped and the sun had set. She nudged Lux awake. "The storm is gone," she whispered, "but it's already night and really dark outside. How are we going to find our way home?"

It was a moonless night, and the clouds that were lingering around after the storm now blocked the stars. It was the darkest sky the sisters had ever seen.

Rubbing the sleep from her eyes, Lux looked up into pitch blackness of the cave and glanced into the eerie darkness outside. She said to Scura in a nervous voice, "I... I think we may need to spend the night here. If we try to go home, we're bound to get lost."

"Lux... I'm scared. It's so dark," Scura said as she huddled closer to her sister.

"Me, too," Lux answered. "We'll be okay if we just stay together."

As if sensing their fear, a soft red, almost pink light began to glimmer toward the back of the cave. Since they were facing the cave's opening, Lux and Scura didn't notice it at first. As the light grew brighter, Lux was startled by faint shadows dancing on the cavern walls. She jumped at the sight.

"Scura, look!" Lux said.

"What *is* that?" Scura replied, seeing the shadows and the warm light for herself.

Sharing her sister's confusion, Lux remained silent. But, the light *did* remind her of something. She just couldn't put her finger on what it was.

With all the excitement of the sudden, torrential storm and the mad run to the cave, Lux had completely forgotten that it was only yesterday since she had visited her friends Rafa and Michael.

Rafa and Michael Miele were the village's beekeepers, harvesting the sweetest and most amazing honey from their hives. However, more importantly (right now at least), their bees also made something else that was very special, a wax that the two gents turned into candles.

"Oh, yes! The candles!" Lux reminded herself.

Lux rummaged frantically through her bag, looking for a particularly large candle Rafa and Michael had made especially for her.

Finally finding it, Lux held the candle above her head like a trophy.

"Yes!" she shouted.

Feeling the overwhelming weight of the inky darkness surrounding them, Scura wasted no time and struck a piece of metal against the rock floor, making a spark and lighting the candle. After a couple of attempts, she managed to create a spark strong enough to light the candle.

Her spirits now buoyed by the glowing light of their candle, Lux stared past her sister to the faint beacon in the cave's depths, finding herself strangely drawn to its rosy glow. She said, almost in a whisper, "It's so beautiful, Scura. Let's go see where that light is coming from."

"Okay," Scura responded, feeling the same urge to find the source of the mysterious light as her sister.

Walking hand in hand, Lux and Scura slowly, carefully ventured deeper into the cave.

As they got drew closer to the source of the light, the ruby glow got brighter and brighter. Their earlier fear forgotten, the sisters forged ahead to the very back of the cave, driven by a newfound need deep within their hearts, a need to find the light.

"There it is!" cried out Scura. She extended her arm and pointed ahead, singling out a crystal on the cave's damp floor. It was about the size and shape of the chestnuts their father would roast for them every fall. This one, solid crystal was perfectly split into two colors, one half clear like a diamond and the other half onyx black. It was alight with a raspberry-colored glow, bathing them in enough light that their candle was no longer needed.

Lux set their candle onto a stone ledge above the shimmering crystal.

"Oh, it's absolutely amazing," Scura said.

"It's the most beautiful thing I've ever seen," Lux said in awe. "If it wasn't for that storm, we never could have found this together. She turned her head to her sister, "I'm so happy to share this with you, Scura."

Scura hadn't even heard her sister speak. She reached out and picked up the mystical gem, taking a closer look. Her gaze had become lost in the stone's beauty.

"Scura, are you okay?" Lux asked, concerned by the odd and intense way her sister was staring at the gem. She put a hand on her sister's shoulder to try to get her attention.

Anger flashed across Scura's face, and she swatted Lux's hand away.

"Don't touch it! It's mine!" Scura shouted with a rage Lux had never seen from her sister. Lux gasped when she saw her sister's normally blue eyes had changed color. They were now a deep violet, so dark they were almost black.

"Stay away!" Scura warned.

Scura stepped back away from Lux, turning her shoulders to keep her body between her sister and the crystal.

As she retreated away, Scura's foot slipped on the loose gravel at the edge of the hole. Neither sister had seen it when they'd first approached their prize, but there was a deep pit in the floor of the cave. A second later, Scura was falling into it, throwing the crystal into the air.

Caring more about her sister than the crystal, Lux dove across the cave and caught Scura's hand just as she'd tumbled over the edge.

"Don't worry! I won't let you fall!" Lux grunted, as she struggled to pull her sister out of the mouth of the seemingly bottomless pit.

Lux struggled and strained and pulled, never loosening the grip on her sister's wrist. It almost felt like the pit was fighting her, trying to claim her sister for its depths. But, inch by inch, she fought to save her sister.

Finally, after what felt like forever, Scura reached her other hand over the edge, and, together, the two sisters hauled Scura to safety.

Lux rested on the floor of the cave, breathless and sweaty from the effort.

"Where is it?" Scura said.

"Where's what?" gasped Lux, dazed after the chaos of just a moment ago.

"The crystal! Where is it?" Scura snapped in frustration as she frantically searched around the cave.

Worrying that the pit wasn't the only danger to her sister, Lux got to her feet and said, "Scura, you're scaring me. We'll find it. Don't worry."

Scura simply ignored her and continued looking for the crystal.

Out of the corner of her eye, Lux saw the telltale red glow coming from under a small pile of rocks that were knocked lose in the struggle to save Scura. Lux crouched down and retrieved the still shimmering gem.

"It's right here. I have it. It's okay, Scura. See?" Lux said.

Scura hurriedly tried to snatch the crystal from her sister's hand. But, in her fury to hold the glowing gem again, she missed. Instead of grabbing it, she sent the crystal flying toward the cave wall.

The crystal smashed against the rock wall. The very instant it hit, a blinding red light filled the cave. The crimson flash faded in a moment, leaving a gem that was no longer glowing nor still in one piece. The crystal had broken into two, identical, heart-shaped halves; one landing near Lux and the other near Scura.

With a darkness in her eyes even scarier than the raging storm that brought the sisters to the cave earlier that day, Scura picked up the half of the crystal that had landed at her feet. Despite her concern for what she was seeing in her sister, Lux slowly bent down to retrieve her half.

As each sister held her own heart-shaped gem, something began to happen. A pitch-black mist began to circle Scura, swirling outward from inside her onyx half of her crystal. At the same time, pure white light shone from the diamond side of Lux's gem, surrounding her.

Through their robes of light and darkness, Lux and Scura stared into each other's eyes, each beginning to understand what destiny had planned for them.

A moment later, silence filled the cave. Both sisters and their crystal hearts were gone, leaving an empty cave with only the light from a single candle to hold away the darkness.

· · · · ·

The Very Beginning...

BAKERSTOWN, PRESENT DAY

Let me tell you a story.

This is a story about a little girl named Rosie Petunia and her adventures... or should I say *misadventures*?

Yes, I think *misadventures* is a much better word. Don't you agree?

Well, I guess you wouldn't know. I haven't told you the story yet. You'll just have to trust me, then, that this tale is better called the *Misadventures of Rosie Petunia.*

It all starts at the "very beginning," as these stories generally do. It was springtime in the small mountain village of Bakerstown. Spring happens to be the best time of year in Bakerstown, but probably not for the reasons you think.

Sure, the flowers are blooming, the birds are singing and the sun is shining, but that's all lame compared to the real reason spring is everyone's favorite season. Every spring, the village holds the Bakerstown Baking Competition.

Yes, I know it's awfully convenient that a town named *Bakers*town holds a famous baking competition. But, what do you want from me? It's not like I made that up for a story. It just happens that a lot of bakers like to compete in Bakerstown.

Anyhoo... the Bakerstown Baking Competition is quite a big deal. Each year bakers come from all the nearby villages and towns to take part in the competition. Mr. Roggen brings his world-famous breads all the way from the neighboring town of Brot. (He's famous for his cinnamon-raisin bread with frosting).

Elisse Biscotto bakes the world's best sugar cookies in the big city of Zucker. Everyone is always exited to try a few. Well, maybe more than a few, but they're just way too tasty.

When it comes to excitement, no one matches Ms. Abigail Pennybottom's magical cupcakes. Those things are incredible. So incredible, in fact, that every year for the past ten years, Ms. Pennybottom has brought home the blue ribbon for first place.

Last year, it was the Chocolate-Fudge Mega-Cake. The year before that, Strawberry Vanilla Surprise. And, no one will ever forget the Blueberry Chocolate Dream from three years ago — rich chocolate cake with a lemon curd center and blueberry frosting. Everybody still talks about it.

The list goes on and on. The deliciousness of her baked treats is unmatched, except, maybe, by her rival Mademoiselle Charlotte Patisserie.

Every time Ms. Pennybottom has taken first-place in the Bakerstown Baking Competition, Mlle.

Patisserie has come in a very close second. Mlle. Patisserie really, really doesn't like that. Not at all.

But, like I said, Ms. Pennybottom's cupcakes are magical, and magic is one doozy of a secret ingredient. Seriously, who can compete with magic?

If your secret ingredient was nutmeg, or cardamom, or even cayenne pepper, I could understand. But, magic? No way.

This year, Mlle. Patisserie has had enough. She has some sneaky tricks of her own hidden in her apron pocket. Are they as magical as Ms. Pennybottom's? You'll have to wait to find out.

Want to know a secret? This year her cupcakes are actually made of magic, and Ms. Pennybottom has no idea. She's in store for a bit of secret magic from a very special friend that she hasn't even met.

But, she'll find out soon enough.

Yes, yes. I know I haven't mentioned Rosie Petunia yet. But, you'll meet her in due time. Be patient. We have to get the right ingredients together. We don't want her introduction to be half-baked.

1

The Actual Beginning...

Now that we've gotten through the very beginning, let's start the story.

Allow me to set the scene for you. Picture this...

It's nighttime, two days before the annual Bakerstown Baking Competition. The mountain air is cool with a touch of warmth on the breeze hinting at the approaching summer.

Ms. Pennybottom is sitting at the counter in the cozy kitchen of her red brick cottage contemplating her recipe for this year's cupcake.

After setting a kettle on the antique potbelly stove to boil water for tea (which helps her think), Ms. Pennybottom glances over at her pet mouse, Napoleon, who is sitting in a copper measuring cup he's claimed as his own. He's licking his lips and eagerly staring at the nearby tray of fresh brownies.

"Hmm," she ponders aloud. "Last year was chocolate. The year before that was strawberry...

She turns to Napoleon who is trying to sneakily thieve a chunk of brownie and asks, "What do we make this year?"

In preparation for the big competition, Ms. Pennybottom has spent the last few days collecting the freshest, rarest and best ingredients she could find, hoping to be inspired.

All of those ingredients are sitting on the kitchen counter, waiting to be chosen as the star of this year's winning cupcake.

There's cinnamon from Armin the Spice Guy, peaches from Georgia who owns a nearby orchard, milk chocolate imported all the way from Choklad, and hazelnuts from a tree in Ms. Pennybottom's own yard.

Looking over her selection of tasty treats, Ms. Pennybottom's eyes widen as she sees a basket of fresh, plump, bright-red raspberries she picked from the woods behind her house sharing a box with a couple of lemons that are twice the size of Napoleon.

The solution to her problem hits her like a pie in the face. Raspberries and lemons — the perfect pairing. It'll be particularly special because lemons are out of season in Bakerstown. Ms. Pennybottom's friend, Citro, shipped her some from the southern city of Karaka, where they grow all year long.

"Perfect!" she shouts a bit too loudly as inspiration strikes, startling Napoleon enough to drop the chunk of brownie he'd stolen when Ms. Pennybottom wasn't looking.

"This year, I'll make lemon cupcakes with raspberry jam center, and raspberry buttercream frosting," she decides. "We'll call them Rosie Raspberry Sensations."

Ms. Pennybottom can't help but name her cupcakes every year. Once, when someone asked her why, she replied,

"Everything you love should have a name, don't you think? I happen to love cupcakes."

Ms. Pennybottom says, expectantly, "I can taste them already. I think these will be great!"

Apparently so can Napoleon, since he manages to look away from his brownie bite just long enough to eagerly nod his head in agreement.

Confident in her decision, Ms. Pennybottom turns to Napoleon and says,

"Now that that's settled, it's late. Time for bed! We'll get started on our Rosie cupcakes bright and early tomorrow at the crack of noon."

Yep. Noon. Ms. Pennybottom is more of a night owl (the clock has just struck 2:30 a.m., as a matter of fact) and doesn't like to wake up too early. Napoleon, for his part, is a well-fed and quite spoiled mouse. He's happy to sleep most of the day, as long has he has breaks for food.

• • • • •

BAKERSTOWN FARMERS MARKET, TWO YEARS AGO

This is probably a good time in the story to explain how Ms. Pennybottom and Napoleon came to be such good friends.

One cold winter day, a few years ago, Ms. Pennybottom was out shopping for ingredients to make apple strudel (which happens to be the perfect dessert for a cold winter day). She'd already collected all of the ingredients she needed, except for the apples.

As she walked into the Bakerstown Farmers Market, she witnessed quite the commotion. Georgia, the local orchard owner and purveyor of the finest apples in Bakerstown, was running around her stall swinging frantically at something with a broom.

"Get back here, you little vermin!" Georgia shouted as she took another swipe with her broom.

After taking in the spectacle in front of her, Ms. Pennybottom called out, "Georgia! What on earth is wrong? What *are* you doing?"

"Oh, sorry, I didn't see you there, Abigail," Georgia replied, breathlessly.

"It's...it's just this stupid mouse. He keeps taking bites out of my fruit!" she cried, looking utterly exasperated as she motioned to the fruit stand next to her.

Ms. Pennybottom walked over to Georgia's fruit stand to see that several of the very apples she'd come to buy had small, rodent-like bits taken out of them.

Then, out of the corner of her eye, she caught sight of a small gray mouse trembling near the base of one of the displays, a look of terror in his eyes.

Ms. Pennybottom walked slowly over to the little fella saying, "Shhh. It's okay. I won't hurt you."

"Georgia," she said to her friend, still gazing down at the mouse, "It's freezing outside. He's just cold and hungry. You can't blame the tiny guy for wanting a little warmth and a bite to eat."

With that Ms. Pennybottom reached out with her open hand, and the little mouse cautiously sniffed her fingers for a few seconds. After coming to the conclusion that this giant, smiling lady wasn't going to hurt him (unlike the meanie with the broom), he climbed up her arm and perched on Ms. Pennybottom's shoulder.

"See. He's just a friendly little mouse," Ms. Pennybottom said to Georgia.

"Alright, little fella...Will you be my friend?" Mrs. Pennybottom asked the mouse who nodded timidly in reply.

"Ok, then. Let's go home, and I'll give you some food and a nice toasty place to sleep."

"Don't worry," she added. "The broom will stay in the closet."

She bought the apples she came for, even the ones with mouse-bites, said her good-byes to Georgia, and left the market.

Back at home, Ms. Pennybottom set her new friend on the kitchen table with a mouse-sized banquet of cheese, bread, cake and the apples had she just bought from Georgia.

"You need a name, little guy," Ms. Pennybottom said to the mouse.

"Let's see... You're tiny, willing to invade people's fruit stands, and would probably look good in an itty-bitty hat," she mused.

"I know," she decided. "I'll call you Napoleon."

Napoleons (the pastry) also happen to be one of Ms. Pennybottom's delicious specialties.

Ever since that day, Ms. Pennybottom and Napoleon have been the best of friends. He's always at her side, joyfully traveling everywhere with her — even to the farmers market. Although, every time they visit Georgia's fruit stand, Napoleon sticks his tongue out at her and shakes his teeny fists.

• • • • •

BAKERSTOWN, TWO DAYS FROM THE BAKING COMPETITION

Meanwhile, across town, pacing back and forth across a starkly lit, modern kitchen of stone and steel, a tall woman with bright white hair, jet black eyes, and all the warmth of a marble slab is hatching a plan for her own competition cupcakes — only her plan is anything but sweet.

"I can't let Pennybottom beat me again this year!" Mlle. Patisserie grouses, as her minions Edgar, a raven, and Toulouse, a cat, look on, more surly than interested.

Toulouse and Edgar are minions, not pets. Pets are family. Mlle. Patisserie sees them merely as tools to do her dirty work, and family wouldn't be told to do what Mlle. Patisserie is about to tell Edgar and Toulouse to do.

"No matter what I do, Pennybottom's cupcakes always win!" Mlle. Patisserie complained.

"I do chocolate, she does chocolate fudge. I make blueberry cupcakes, she adds lemon curd!" she continues, bitterly. "I've had enough!"

"No more!" she exclaims, slamming her fist on the counter, making Toulouse and Edgar nearly hit the ceiling in fright.

Staring directly at her minions, Mlle. Patisserie says,

"Instead of just baking my cupcakes and hoping I can out-do Pennybottom, I'll send you two over to spy on her and report back to me with her recipe," she explained. "Then I'll know exactly what to bake to take first prize!"

With a cold, cruel stare, Mlle. Patisserie warns her minions, "Don't fail me."

Edgar and Toulouse nod shakily in agreement and slink out of the room. Well...Toulouse slinks, Edgar just flies.

"This year, I can't lose," she says tenting her fingers like a cartoon villain.

Outside Mlle. Patisserie's kitchen window, a pair of bright violet eyes peer through the darkness, watching her as she hatches her plan. The mouth that sits just below the violet stare curls into a cruel, approving smile.

Little does Mlle. Patisserie know, there's someone else who wants her to beat Ms. Pennybottom even more than she does.

There's more at stake in this year's baking competition than just a blue ribbon. Neither Ms. Pennybottom or Mlle. Patisserie have any idea what's in store for them.

2

A Surprise Gift...

The next day (sometime around noon), Ms. Pennybottom and Napoleon are sitting at the kitchen table enjoying a nice breakfast of raspberry scones with boysenberry jam and coffee when they hear a knock at the door.

Annoyed that someone would interrupt his meal, Napoleon lets out a frustrated sigh. Ms. Pennybottom is less protective of her mealtime and cheerily wonders who's at the door.

Peeking through the lace curtain, Ms. Pennybottom recognizes her neighbor Hector Pantalones, the town tailor. He's also the person Ms. Pennybottom has had a crush on for quite some time.

• • • • •

BAKERSTOWN, THREE WEEKS FROM THE BAKING COMPETITION

Hector moved to Bakerstown a few weeks ago from the city of Tailleur on the other side of the mountain to open a tailor shop. He bought the house two doors down from Ms. Pennybottom as the old owner was moving to Zucker to start a new job as a dog groomer.

Ms. Pennybottom noticed the moving van in front of her neighbor's house.

"I wonder who's moving into Koira's old house," she thought to herself.

Since she is the premier baker of Bakerstown, Ms. Pennybottom saw it as her duty to make her new neighbor a welcome-to-the-neighborhood plate of chocolate chip and toffee cookies.

The next day, after the moving van had gone, Ms. Pennybottom knocked on the door of her new neighbor. A man's voice shouted from inside,

"Hello! I'm coming. Just buried in boxes and bubble wrap at the moment. I'll be right there!"

Ms. Pennybottom heard the sound of cardboard boxes sliding across a hardwood floor and several *pop-pop-pops*, which she could only assume was the noise of a man trying to get out of a huge pile of bubble wrap.

Seriously, though, who doesn't love popping bubble wrap.

A few moments later, the lock unlatched and a tall, handsome man with wavy, dark brown hair, kind green eyes, and a bushy beard opened the door.

He was wearing jeans and a Sastre University t-shirt and looked a bit disheveled, which was no surprise since he was busy unpacking an entire house.

"Hey. Can I help you?" the man said.

Ms. Pennybottom took a second to respond. For some reason, she was bit flustered all of a sudden.

"Hi," she finally squeaked out.

Recovering her wits, she continued,

"My name is Abigail Pennybottom. I live in the cottage two doors down, and I wanted to be the first to welcome you to the neighborhood," she said handing over the plate of cookies.

"Cookies, awesome! Thanks a lot. I'm Hector Pantalones," Hector said. "I just moved in."

As soon as the words left his mouth, Hector thought to himself, "Bonehead. Of course, she knows you just moved in. There are boxes everywhere, and she brought you welcome cookies. Get your head together, Pantalones!"

Hector, too, was feeling a bit flustered upon seeing the lovely woman with bright pink hair, chocolate brown eyes and just a little bit of baking flour on her shoes (no doubt from the cookies).

"They're chocolate chip and toffee. I hope you like them," Ms. Pennybottom said sincerely, shrugging her shoulders.

"Actually, they're my favorite," Hector answered.

Finally getting it together, Hector said,

"I would love to invite you in for cookies and a cup of coffee, but I have no idea where my coffee, coffee pot, or coffee cups are at the moment."

Ms. Pennybottom laughed and said, "No problem. I understand. Moving is the worst."

"Next time," Hector promised.

"Next time," Ms. Pennybottom agreed. "I guess I'll see you around the neighborhood."

"I hope so, Abigail," Hector admitted. "Thanks again for the cookies".

"You're welcome. Good luck unpacking. Bye," Ms. Pennybottom said with twinkling eyes as she turned to head back to her house.

"Bye!" Hector said as she stepped off his front porch.

"Wow!" Hector said to himself as he closed the door and decided it was a good time for a cookie break.

"Wow!" Ms. Pennybottom said to Napoleon as soon as she entered through her front door.

Napoleon just looked at her, shrugged his shoulders and went back to his camembert snack.

• • • • •

BAKERSTOWN, ONE DAY FROM THE BAKING COMPETITION

Today, instead of his usual tailor's smock and rolled-up sleeves, Hector is wearing a perfectly-fitting gray tweed blazer, dark blue jeans, a white shirt with gray polka dots and black shoes so polished you could see the reflection of the petunias Ms. Pennybottom planted in her yard.

Ms. Pennybottom smiles broadly and blushes when she sees Hector. You see, while Ms. Pennybottom has really liked Hector since the day she met him a few weeks ago, she's been a bit too shy to say much of anything to him since then. So, the surprise of seeing him at her door made her very happy but also very nervous.

What she didn't know is that Hector felt the exact same way. It took him over an hour to get over his nerves enough to knock on her door.

A couple of days ago, Hector saw Ms. Pennybottom shopping at the local market. He wanted to go over to say hello, but that time his nerves got the better of him.

He decided the best way to break the ice with Ms. Pennybottom was to give her a good-luck-gift for the big baking competition, returning the favor of the cookies she gave him when he moved in.

Straightening her sundress and smoothing her bright pink hair, Ms. Pennybottom musters her strength, opens the door and says in greeting, "Good morning, er, afternoon Hector. How nice to see you!"

Hector replies, "And, good afternoon to you, Abigail."

"I know the big competition is tomorrow, and I'm sure you must be hard at work coming up with your next bit of bakery magic."

He continues a bit sheepishly, "I just wanted to stop by and give you a little good luck gift."

"A gift? You shouldn't have!" Ms. Pennybottom replies as Hector hands her a box beautifully wrapped in yellow and purple striped paper with a big orange bow.

"But, since you did, thank you!" she says smoothly, even though inside her heart and stomach were doing somersaults.

Untying the bow and giddily tearing off the paper, Mrs. Pennybottom finds the loveliest, most useful, and most darling apron she's ever seen nestled inside the box.

The apron is the same color pink as her hair, with big green dots, two huge pockets and her name embroidered in purple near the top.

"I hope you like it. I made it just for you." Hector says softly, a bit unsure.

"Like it? I love it!" Ms. Pennybottom answers, forgetting any of her earlier shyness. "It's perfect. I'll wear it every day."

Hector smiles the biggest smile Ms. Pennybottom had ever seen.

"Would you like to come in for a cup of coffee and some scones, if Napoleon hasn't eaten them all?" Ms. Pennybottom offers.

"I would love to," Hector accepts, fulfilling the promise of *next time* they made when they first met. "But, who's Napoleon?"

"Hector, allow me to introduce my faithful assistant and good friend Napoleon the Mouse," Ms. Pennybottom says with a flair of formality.

Setting down a piece of scone that was nearly as large as his head, Napoleon scampers over to Hector and offered his paw.

Hector laughs and shakes the tiny mouse's hand.

"Pleased to meet you, Napoleon. May I join you for scones?" Hector asks, equally formally.

Napoleon nods and turns to Ms. Pennybottom, winks and gives her a thumbs up.

Hector and Ms. Pennybottom sit in her living room, talking and laughing. The shyness and nervousness are gone, and they become very comfortable with each other. They became so comfortable and had so much fun talking that Ms. Pennybottom completely loses track of time.

All of a sudden *Bong. Bong. Bong.* The grandfather clock in the living room chimes.

"Wow. Is it three o'clock, already?" Ms. Pennybottom says with a start.

"I didn't realize it was so late," Hector says. "I'm sure you have a lot to do before tomorrow."

Ms. Pennybottom replies, "I really should get to work. Thank you again for the lovely apron. It was great talking to you, Hector."

Hector says, "You're very welcome, and it really was. I hope we can do it again."

"Me, too," Ms. Pennybottom says, very quickly.

Hector smiled and says, "Well, I guess I better let you get back to your baking."

Ms. Pennybottom walks Hector to the front door where they say their goodbyes.

As he walks back home, Hector is smiling the whole way.

Also smiling quite largely, Ms. Pennybottom puts on her new apron. Buoyed by her wonderful afternoon with Hector, she's ready to get to work.

"What do you think, Napoleon?"

He answers emphatically, "Squeak! Squeeeak squeeeeaaak!"

Now, I don't speak very good mouse, but I think *"Squeak! Squeeeak squeeeeaaak!"* means "It looks great! Now let's get to work!"

Almost immediately the little mouse heads over to the sink to start washing raspberries, which I believe confirms my translation.

3

Magic in the Mountains...

CASTLE DOIS, ONE DAY FROM THE BAKING COMPETITION

High above Bakerstown towers Mount Jadu. Near the summit of the snow-capped mountain flows the river Magia. Bridging both sides of the river is the magnificent Castle Dois.

Castle Dois isn't your average castle. There is a straight line running from top to bottom splitting the castle into two halves; one side made of gold and the other side of onyx.

The golden half shimmers in the sunlight, casting a warm glow. The onyx half is in constant shadow, draining the light from everything around it.

Since from the outside Castle Dois looks like one building with two very different halves, it makes sense that everything inside the castle also follows the same pattern, with gold and onyx materials filling each side. Everything, that is, except for one long room at the top of highest tower.

This room is a long and narrow rectangle with a high ceiling and tall windows along each of the longest walls. Walk along the two longest walls and at the exact center you'll find shining gold give way to deep black onyx where the two halves of the castle meet. There are two entrances into the room, a single door at either end.

The room is empty except for a long rectangular table running perfectly down the center of the room. The table is made of the purest, most perfect gold. At each end of the table rests a single chair; one onyx, the other diamond.

I'll let you figure out which chair is on which side.

Twin sisters sit in the priceless chairs. Though they are twins, the sisters don't look exactly alike. The sister sitting in the diamond chair has platinum white hair, sky-blue eyes and seems almost to be glowing. She's wearing a pearl-white gown, and around her neck hangs a gold chain with a diamond and onyx amulet.

The sister sitting in the onyx chair bears a similar appearance, but she has jet black hair, violet eyes and (if it's even possible) seems to be in constant shadow. She wears a dark purple gown, with a platinum chain holding an onyx and diamond amulet.

Both sisters are silently staring into a huge magical crystal ball that is perched on a diamond stand in the exact center of the golden table.

Images of Ms. Pennybottom and Mlle. Patisserie hard at work in their kitchens dance across the surface of the sphere.

As they watch what's happening far below in Bakerstown, one sister finds herself lost in memory, returning to a time before the castle, before the gold and the onyx...before the magic.

· · · · ·

THE FUTURE SITE OF BAKERSTOWN, 999 YEARS AGO

A long, long time ago (nine-hundred and ninety-nine years to be precise), twin sisters lived in a small village that sat exactly where Bakerstown can be found today. They were happy and playful kids. They were also very close, as only twins can be. They did everything together.

On glorious sunny days the sisters loved playing tag in the woods behind their family's cottage and challenging each other at board games when it was rainy.

Every summer, they spent the long, warm days swimming in the river and picking berries for their favorite activity, baking.

One particularly lovely May morning, the twins were strolling around the nearby woods collecting berries to use in a pie when they heard a strange sound coming from deep within the forest. It sounded like the jingling of dozens of crystal windchimes. It was musical, almost magical, to the girls' ears.

Feeling a strong pull toward the noise, one of the twins, Cerise, turned off the trail they were following to try to find the source of the melody. Her sister, Juniper, reached out to stop her as their parents had warned them from wandering too far from the path.

"Mom and Dad told us not to leave the trail," Juniper warned.

"Come on June," Cerise urged. "Don't you want to see where that sound is coming from?"

"But, we're supposed to stay on the path," Juniper answered, even though she herself was feeling the same pull toward the sound that her sister was.

"Listen to it," Cerise continued. "It's the most beautiful thing I've ever heard! I need to see where it's coming from!"

With that, Cerise pulled away from her sister and ran off into the trees in search of the source.

"Ceri! Wait!" Juniper shouted. "Ceri!"

But, Cerise ignored her and kept running, following the sound of the chimes. Afraid to leave her sister alone in the woods, Juniper gave in and shouted, "Wait up! I'm coming too!" as she set off after her twin sister.

Moments later, Juniper caught up with Cerise when she stopped at a humongous willow tree growing in the middle of a clearing in the forest. Both girls' mouths dropped open at what they saw.

Hanging from the ancient tree were hundreds of shining crystal windchimes. Each one moved in the breeze, making the hypnotic music that drew in the girls.

All of a sudden, the wind stopped, and the chimes grew silent. There was a sudden flash, so bright that Juniper and Cerise had to cover their eyes with their hands.

Then, a soft, gentle voice spoke.

"Hello my dears," the voice said, the words sounding like they were coming from all around the twins, even though no one else was there.

"Um... H-h-hello," Juniper replied, unsteadily.

"We have waited a long time for you to find this place," said the voice.

"Yeah. I've been getting tired of waiting. About time you got here," a second voice chided.

The second voice wasn't as gentle or as kind as the first. It was harsh with a cruel edge that frightened the girls.

Juniper and Cerise look at each other, nervous and confused at what the voices were saying.

Cerise spoke up. "What do you mean you've been waiting for us? Who are you?"

The first voice responded, her voice seemingly coming from the sunlight that lit the valley. "We are the Keepers of Magic. We guard the Balance of the Light and the Dark and have been doing so for three thousand years."

The voice continued, "You may call me Keeper of the Light."

"Yeah, I'm Keeper of the Dark. I'm ready to retire," the second voice interrupted from the shadows.

"Long ago, Juniper and Cerise, you were chosen as the next Keepers of Magic," the first voice explained. "You were destined to find us here."

Cerise and Juniper had trouble believing the Keepers of Magic, but hearing voices that came from nowhere and seeing a giant tree covered in glowing crystal windchimes did quite a bit to convince the twins they weren't crazy, especially since they both saw and heard the same things.

"How could we possibly be the new...you?" Juniper asked in disbelief. "We're just kids and we don't have any magic."

"You'll be tested, you fool," the Keeper of the Dark said, rudely. "One day each of you will make a choice that will decide who takes my job as Keeper of the Dark and who takes over for Miss Goody-Good with the light stuff."

"Until then, my children, be well" the Keeper of the Light said.

Another blinding flash of light stunned Juniper and Cerise. When they opened their eyes, they found themselves back on the path where they started, each with full baskets of berries for their pie.

"That was weird," Cerise noted. "But, at least they gave us berries. That was nice of them."

• • • • •

ON THE FUTRE SITE OF BAKERSTOWN, 999 YEARS AGO

After that day in the forest, the girls went on with their life as before. Summers came and went, but the words of the Keepers of Magic were never far from their minds.

Years passed as Juniper and Cerise grew into teenagers and then into adults. Though years had passed the sister remained very close, living together in a small house just down the road from their parents. They even opened a bakery together, turning their favorite hobby into a job they both loved very, very much.

One day, Cerise was walking back from the mill with a bag of flour for their shop when she passed the town message board. There she saw a flyer for the town's first baking competition. First prize offered a trip to the capital city, where the winning baked good would be served at a royal banquet.

"A baking competition! I can't believe it!" thought Cerise as a dream of serving her food at a royal banquet made her more excited than she's ever been.

She ran home as fast as she could to tell her sister the great news.

"June! June! Guess what! There's a baking competition and first prize is a trip to the capital and a ticket to a royal banquet where they'll serve the winning entry!" Cerise shouted as she burst through their front door.

"What? That's amazing, Ceri!" Juniper replied, equally excited. "What should we make? How about a cake? No... cinnamon rolls. Or, maybe..."

"Hold on, June. The rules on the sign said individual entries only," Cerise said. "That means we each have to make something to enter."

"Oh," Juniper said, a bit sadly. "Well, may the best sister win! Good luck, Ceri!" Ever since they could remember, Juniper and Cerise did everything together. This would be the first time they would compete against each other.

"Thanks. You too, June!" Cerise replied. But, in the privacy of her mind, Cerise thought there was no way her sister could beat her. After all, Cerise was sure she was the better baker.

The day before the competition, Cerise was sitting in the living room thinking about her entry. She had made the most perfect cherry pie. Golden, flaky crust. Bright red cherry filling that was sweet but with just the right amount of tartness. It was the best thing she'd ever made. She was ready to win. She was sure of it.

"Hey Ceri, want to see what I made?" Juniper called from the kitchen, interrupting Cerise as she was mentally writing her acceptance speech.

Cerise walked into the kitchen to see a five-layer almond cake with meringue, apricots and candied slivers of almonds. It looked delicious and smelled even better. Much to Cerise's dismay, it was perfect.

Cerise knew at that moment, no matter how good her pie was, her sister's cake was better. She became very, very angry.

"It looks amazing," Cerise forced herself to say through gritted teeth.

"It took all week, but it's finally done." Juniper said. Exhausted, she headed upstairs to bed. "Tomorrow is the big day and I need some rest. Good night, Ceri."

"Night, June," Cerise responded absentmindedly, her mind reeling at the thought that she might lose.

Cerise just sat there, staring at this flawless cake, getting madder and madder.

"I can't lose. I won't lose," she said to herself. And, in a fit of rage, she threw her sister's cake across the kitchen, believing that if Juniper had no entry, she would win.

As soon as Juniper's cake hit the wall, a familiar blinding light flashed throughout the twins' house. Juniper and Cerise found themselves back in the same clearing in front of the same willow with the same crystal chimes hearing the same magical melody.

"Told you that you'd be tested," the Keeper of the Dark said, her voice no less cruel and frightening than it was all those years ago.

"What? What test?" Juniper asked, quite confused as to what was going on.

"Ask your sister," the Keeper of the Dark answered.

"Ceri, what's she talking about?" Juniper said, suddenly terrified that her life was about to dramatically change.

"I....I couldn't let you win," Ceri replied.

"Win? Win what? Wait, you mean the baking competition? What did you do?" Juniper questioned.

"I threw your cake at the wall. I deserve to win more than you. I'm the better baker," Ceri admitted without a hint of shame or guilt.

"Why would you do that? It's just a dumb competition," Juniper said. "If it was so important to you, you should have just told me. I wouldn't have entered. No competition is that important."

"Dumb competition?!? Dumb?!?" Cerise shouted. "This competition is everything!"

Juniper just stared, shocked at what she was hearing. She'd never seen this side of her twin sister.

"By destroying Juniper's cake, Cerise has betrayed her sister. She broke the Balance, betrayed the Light, and chose the Dark," the Keeper of the Light explained.

"She has revealed her true self. The decision has been made. Juniper, you will be the Keeper of the Light. Cerise you will be the Keeper of the Dark."

The Keeper of the Dark added. "Cerise, as a consequence of your betrayal, the person you were is no more. You're changed. The person you were — the self you've always known is dead. Your name is no longer Cerise. You will now be known as Bruxa Mala."

• • • • •

On that day, nine-hundred and ninety-nine years ago, the Keepers of the Magic passed on their powers to Juniper and Cerise, now named Bruxa Mala.

Just like everything in life, magic has a good side and an evil side. A light side and a dark side. Juniper became a good witch, the Keeper of the Light. Bruxa Mala became a dark witch, the Keeper of the Dark.

Since they were twins charged with keeping the Balance between the Light and the Dark, Juniper and Bruxa Mala's powers were linked to each other. One could not exist without the other. They were forced by the laws of magic to remain together for the next three thousand years, after which time they are to pass their powers to the next pair of Keepers.

Bruxa Mala's love for her sister faded more and more over the centuries. Eventually, she stopped caring about her sister and the Balance. She only craved power. She wanted to win. She began searching for a way to tip the Balance.

Bruxa Mala started challenging her sister and the Light, hoping to finally win and rule the world in darkness. Her goal was to prove what she began believing centuries ago, that she was the greater sister.

The rules of magic that I mentioned before also prevented Bruxa Mala from attacking her sister directly. Any attack one sister threw at the other would strike them back just as hard. So, they used others to fight their battles. One such battle was just beginning in Bakerstown.

No one knew it yet, but this battle was going to be different.

· · · · ·

CASTLE DOIS, ONE DAY FROM THE BAKING COMPETITION

Her sky-blue eyes never leaving the crystal ball, Juniper quietly says, "I know what you're trying to do, sister. It won't work."

With a laugh, the evil witch replies, "My dear sister, you have no idea what I'm doing."

Bruxa Mala calls out for her apprentice, "Lana, get over here. I have a job for you."

Juniper glances over to her own apprentice, Nata, and wonders what exactly her sister is planning.

4

Not Playing Fair...

BAKERSTOWN, ONE DAY FROM THE BAKING COMPETITION

Meanwhile back in Bakerstown, an onyx-black cat sits on the windowsill outside Ms. Pennybottom's kitchen staring at the activity inside. Just above the window, a raven with cold yellow eyes is perched on a low branch of a nearby hazelnut tree.

In her kitchen, Ms. Pennybottom is happily assembling the ingredients for her Rosie Raspberry Sensation cupcakes.

"Alright, Napoleon, let's go down the list," Ms. Pennybottom says to her itsy-bitsy assistant.

"Raspberries?" she asks.

"Squeak," Napoleon confirms.

(*Squeak*, by the way, means *check*.)

"Lemons?"

"Squeak."

"Flour?"

"Squeak?"

"Eggs, vanilla, milk, butter?"

"Squeak, squeak, squeak, squeak."

"Sugar?"

No response from the mouse.

"Napoleon, sugar?" Ms. Pennybottom asks again.

Napoleon looks around, finally spotting the bag of sugar and responding,

"Squeak!"

"Okay. I think that's everything," Ms. Pennybottom confirms.

"Time to make our Rosie Raspberry Sensations," she proclaims.

"I think these may be just be my best cupcakes yet. The lemon will make all the difference. I hope everyone enjoys them."

Outside, Edgar the Raven and Toulouse the Cat hear all they need to and jump from their perches to return and tell Mlle. Patisserie what they've learned.

. . . . .

"Raspberry and lemon cupcakes!" Mlle. Patisserie screams, throwing a wooden spoon at Edgar and Toulouse.

"How did she even find good lemons this time of year?!?"

Boiling mad, she asks no one in particular, "Ahhh! How can I make something to compete with Pennybottom when I can't even figure out how gets she her ingredients?"

"Maybe I can help," says a voice from the shadows.

Startled, Mlle. Patisserie says angrily, "Who's there? What are you doing in my house?"

A tall woman with fiery red hair and a mischievous grin steps into the light.

"My name is Lana. I'm here representing my master who would like to offer you some assistance to beat Ms. Pennybottom," the tall woman proposes.

"What are you talking about? What do you mean *your master*?" Mlle. Patisserie demands.

Lana holds out a hand and replies, "Let's just say I work for an interested party who would like to see you win."

As she speaks, a box of very red, very ripe cherries appears in Lana's outstretched hand.

Lana says, "As I'm sure you can see, this is a box of perfect cherries. Better than anything available within five-hundred miles of Bakerstown. They are amazing on their own, however, my master has added something... special."

"Special?" Mlle. Patisserie asks, skeptically.

"Special." Lana replies, matter-of-factly.

"Well...Out with it. What's so special about the cherries?" Mlle. Patisserie says, her curiosity peaked.

"Why, they're enchanted, of course." Lana says.

"Anyone who takes even a single bite will be put under a spell. For a full day, anything they eat will taste like garbage. Anything, that is, except for these cherries," Lana explained. "As long as the judges try your dessert before Pennybottom's, you can't lose."

Mlle. Patisserie raises an eyebrow and asks Lana, "What's the catch?"

Shaking her head, Lana answers, "No catch. My master only wants to see you win and Ms. Pennybottom lose."

Mlle. Patisserie reaches out, grabs the box of cherries and says, "Fine. Give me the cherries, and let me get on with my work."

But, as soon as Mlle. Patisserie takes the cherries, Lana disappears from the kitchen without a sound.

Not quite sure what just happened, Mlle. Patisserie has decided to trust her mysterious benefactor and focus on making a cherry tartlet that will finally annihilate Ms. Pennybottom.

She knows exactly what to make... A cherry tartlet.

Mlle. Patisseries is willing to do anything to win, even cheat and accept cherries cursed with dark magic.

• • • • •

Toulouse and Edgar aren't the only spies in Bakerstown. A mane of platinum blond hair surrounding a kind face with keen eyes is unnoticed outside Mlle. Patisserie's kitchen window.

Veiled under a cloak of invisibility magic, Nata, the Keeper of the Light's apprentice, sees the entire exchange between Lana and Mlle. Patisserie. She knows that somehow Bruxa Mala is trying to sway the Balance by helping Mlle. Patisserie beat Ms. Pennybottom. She just doesn't know how exactly.

Nata disappears with a gust of wind, returning to tell Juniper the bad news.

• • • • •

BAKERSTOWN BOARDING SCHOOL 20 YEARS AGO

Bruxa Mala and Juniper know why Mlle. Patisserie hates Ms. Pennybottom so deeply, which is why they're taking such an interest in them and this year's Bakerstown Baking Competition.

You should probably know, too. It's important to the story, after all.

Abigail Pennybottom and Charlotte Patisserie have known each other since they were small. They grew up together in the Bakerstown Boarding School and were the best of friends. As a matter of fact, they were as close as sisters, maybe even as close as twins.

The Bakerstown Boarding School was run by Headmistress Kena. She was a kind and gentle woman who treated the children like they were her own. She loved each and every child in the school.

Running a school was a lot of work. There were meals to prepare, dishes to do, floors to mop, and bathrooms to clean (yuck!). Everyone in the Bakerstown Boarding School had to help out with the daily chores.

Headmistress Kena was fair in assigning chores. Some weeks you were on the dreaded bathroom duty and others you were in charge of watering the garden.

It must be told that watering the garden was a prized chore, as you were allowed to use whatever water-er you wanted, even a squirt-gun or water-balloon (as long as you picked up the popped balloons afterward, of course).

Early on, Abigail and Charlotte were assigned their chores just like everyone else, but it didn't take long for Headmistress Kena to realize that the two girls were very talented at one particular chore. Little Abigail Pennybottom and Charlotte Patisserie were wonderful cooks.

No matter what they were making — salad, main course, side dish, or dessert — it was absolutely delicious. Soon, none of the children in Headmistress Kena's care minded that Abigail and Charlotte never had bathroom duty. Their food was just too good.

Eventually, the friends were assigned permanently to helping in the kitchen. As both girls loved to cook, this made them very happy.

As the years went by, Abigail and Charlotte explored their love of cooking. They adored trying new ingredients and sharing new recipes with each other.

Baking was their absolute favorite. Bread, cookies, pies, cakes... It didn't matter. Both Charlotte and Abigail **LOVED** to bake. Together, they made the tastiest of baked goods.

All of that changed on one fateful day. Charlotte and Abigail had just turned seventeen years old. The next year, they would be leaving the Bakerstown Boarding School and going to a university.

All of their friends had decided what they wanted to do and gotten into the schools they wanted. Abigail and Charlotte knew exactly what they wanted to do, too.

Ever since they were little, the two girls fantasized about going to the prestigious Cuisson Institute to study in their world-renowned Baking Master Program. They even planned on being roommates in the dorms so they could keep sharing recipes.

When the time came, both girls applied to this very competitive program. Both girls were invited to interview with the head of admissions to earn their spot in the school. And, both girls made it all the way to the last step... They had to bake and audition pastry.

The task was simple. Bake something good enough, and you get into the Cuisson Institute Baking Master Program.

However, there was one big problem.

That year, the Baking Master Program only had one open space. Neither Abigail nor Charlotte knew that. As far as they knew, the dream they'd had since they were little was about to come true.

The two girls spent days and days planning the perfect pastry.

"Abs, you're so good at cakes. You really need to make a cupcake," Charlotte suggested.

"I don't know," Abigail replied, unsure. "I'm not sure it'll be enough."

"Don't worry. The way you combine flavors... They'll never see it coming. You'll wow 'em for sure!" Charlotte reassured.

"Maybe you're right," Abigail said. "I'll make a cupcake. I've always loved my cookies and cream recipe. Think that'll work?"

"Definitely!" Charlotte confirmed.

"Thanks, Charry," Abigail said. "What about you? You make the best cherry tartlet I've ever tasted. You should totally make that!"

"That's what I was thinking," Charlotte said. "I'm glad you agree!"

Charlotte and Abigail baked like crazy to whip up two pastries, one cupcake and one tartlet, that they were both quite proud of and ready to submit to the Cuisson Institute.

The next day, the day of the judging, the two friends proudly submitted their pastries, confident in the thought they would both be admitted.

"Abigail Pennybottom. Charlotte Patisserie. Thank you both for your entries," Chef Simon Kolach said. "Both pastries were excellent."

"Unfortunately," he continued, "there is only one spot available in the Baking Master Program this year."

Abigail and Charlotte turned toward each other, shocked. They'd never considered that only one of them would get into the program. With pale faces and wide eyes, they waited for Chef Kolach to finish.

"This was a very difficult decision," he said. "Both of you made wonderful pastries. Charlotte, your tartlet was flaky with a perfect balance of sweet and tart. It was technically flawless."

Charlotte Patisserie flushed with excitement.

"Abigail," Chef Kolach continued. "Your cookies and cream cupcake was moist and tender with a perfect crumb. It was also technically flawless. But, the little hint of vanilla in your fudge center was genius."

Chef Kolach proclaimed, "For your creative use of unexpected flavors, Ms. Abigail Pennybottom, I am proud to offer you a spot at the Cuisson Institute Baking Master Program!"

Abigail beamed. This was everything she'd dreamed of. Well, almost everything. Beside her, Charlotte's eyes became dark with rage and envy.

"You're wrong!" she screamed.

"You're all wrong! I'm the better baker, not this amateur!" she shouted, pointing at Abigail.

"Oh, Charry! I'm so sorry," Abigail said, sincerely.

"SHUT UP!!!" Charlotte yelled and she ran from the room.

Later that afternoon, Abigail knocked on Charlotte's bedroom door. Hearing no reply, she knocked again and inquired,

"Charry? You in there?"

When there was no reply from within, Abigail opened the door to find the room completely emptied of Charlotte's things except for a single photo torn in half sitting on the dresser. The photo showed a smiling Abigail and Charlotte, both covered in flour and holding a wooden spoon and a whisk.

· · · · ·

BAKERSTOWN, THE NIGHT BEFORE THE BAKING
COMPETITION

A kitchen timer that looks like a small, green frog buzzes loudly in Ms. Pennybottom's kitchen, startling Napoleon out of his nap. She rushes over and opens the oven door.

"I think they're done, Napoleon," she says, inspecting the tray of golden lemon cupcakes as she removes them from the oven.

"Yep. Definitely done," she asserts to the mouse as he yawns loudly.

Napoleons yawns are surprisingly noisy considering he's a mouse.

Wiping her hands on her new pink apron, Ms. Pennybottom says, "Once they cool, I'll frost the cupcakes with the raspberry butter cream and we'll be ready for the big day tomorrow."

• • • • •

Beeeep. Beeeep. Beeeep. Across town, Mlle. Patisserie's own kitchen timer goes off. Her timer isn't anything as fun as a frog — it's a gray digital clock that beeps shrilly when the countdown is done.

Mlle. Patisserie pulls her cherry tartlets out of her oven and says to Edgar and Toulouse,

"These look perfect. But, I've made perfect cherry tartlets before and still lost to that dreadful Pennybottom. That Lana woman better be right about these cherries."

Edgar and Toulouse look at each other, terrified at what will happen if Mlle. Patisserie loses.

5

The Big Day...

CASTLE DOIS, THE DAY OF THE BAKING COMPETITION

DAY 1 OF THE TIPPING

"I knew she was up to something," Juniper, the Keeper of the Light, says to her apprentice, Nata.

The Keeper and her apprentice are in Juniper's private study. It's a big, perfectly square room with very tall ceilings on the highest floor of the golden side of Castle Dois. The walls and floor are as white as cake flour, and there are two massive windows with shimmering curtains made of silk spun with pure gold thread.

A single book sits on a solid gold stand in the exact center of the room. Next to the book on its own precious stand is an empty willow wood jewelry box that once held a very special necklace. An identical book and jewelry box sit in the exact center of Bruxa Mala's study.

The two magicians, Juniper and Nata, are sitting in royal blue velvet chairs with tall backs and deep cushions on opposite sides of a fireplace that's so big you could stand in it.

"Enchanted cherries..." she whispers, more to herself than anyone else.

"Why is the baking competition so important this year?" Nata asks.

The question catches Juniper off guard, and she startles a bit having forgotten there was anyone else in the room.

Finding her way back from thoughts of a past so ancient that few remember it ever existed to the present day, she answers, "Long ago, my sister made a cherry pie for a baking competition. I made a cake."

Juniper remembers, "It was the first time we ever competed against each other. Before then, we were an inseparable team."

"She wanted victory more than anything in the world, but she was afraid, terrified I would win. So...she destroyed the cake I'd baked to ensure I couldn't beat her."

Juniper looks at Nata sadly, and says, "My dear sister lost her balance that day and became the Keeper of the Dark. As you know, I became Keeper of the Light. This year's Bakerstown Baking Competition falls on the one-thousandth anniversary of that fateful day."

"A thousand years is a very long time," Nata comments, amazed at how much time as passed since the sisters became the Keepers.

"It feels like an eternity sometimes," Juniper confesses.

She looks at Nata and says, seriously, "It's not just about my sister and me. A millennium is a very special amount of time in magic."

Turning to gaze through the castle's huge window at the town far, far below, Juniper asks her young assistant, "Did you ever wonder why Castle Dois sits above Bakerstown?"

"No, not really," Nata admits.

"There is a line, called the Equalis, that runs down the middle of the world. The world is balanced between good and bad and the Equalis represents that balance," Juniper explains.

She continues, "Only one town in the whole world is split in two equal halves by the Equalis..."

"Bakerstown," Nata says, finishing Juniper's thought.

"Correct, Nata. Very good." Juniper says. "That's why every Keeper throughout history has come from that small spot of land."

Nata looks on, amazed.

"Every thousand years, for one week," Juniper says, "the Balance between Light and Dark is weakened; opened to swaying either way, to good or bad. That week is called the Tipping."

Juniper looks her assistant in the eyes and says, "It starts today."

The Keeper of the Light continues, "Right now, Bakerstown is balanced between Light and Dark, but because of its position on the Equalis, at the end of this week, if Bakerstown turns toward the Dark, so falls the rest of the world."

Juniper stares at Nata with an intensity she's never seen. She then says, direly,

"My sister's one goal for all these past centuries has been to cover the world in darkness. That cannot happen. We must ensure that it does not happen."

For over ten-thousand years, no Keeper of Magic, Light or Dark, has been able to sway the Balance. Let's hope that this year, Bruxa Mala doesn't succeed where all others have failed."

· · · · ·

BAKERSTOWN BAKING COMPETITION

DAY 1 OF THE TIPPING

The day of the Bakerstown Baking Competition was a beautiful day, indeed. The sun was shining. The air was warm. There wasn't a cloud in the sky. All was lovely in the village of Bakerstown.

It's really a good thing that it wasn't raining, since the judges' table for the competition was in the gazebo that marks the center of the Village Square park. Outdoor baking competitions and rain definitely don't mix.

Village Square park is in the precise center of Bakerstown, and the Equalis runs right down the middle of the judges' table. Of course, no one in town realizes this.

Competitors came from far and wide with their most delicious of entries. As usual, Mr. Roggen is in from Brot. This year he brought a particularly delightful looking pumpernickel loaf with golden raisins. Elisse Biscotto is here, too, with a batch of simply wonderful snickerdoodles all the way from Zucker.

Despite the mouth-watering display of tasty baked goods, the biggest attractions are Ms. Pennybottom's Rosie Raspberry Sensation cupcakes (lemon with raspberry buttercream, if you recall) and Mlle. Patisserie's absolutely enchanting (literally) cherry tartlet.

"Wow!" Ms. Pennybottom says to Napoleon and Hector (whom she asked to join her for the day). Everything looks amazing. This has to be the best competition in years."

Hector reassures her, "Don't worry Abby, you got this in the bag."

Napoleon nods eagerly in agreement and fist-bumps Hector.

"I hope so," Ms. Pennybottom replies. "If I don't win this year, it'll be okay because I know I'll have tried my best and lost to some really amazing work by some really amazing bakers. Either way... I still really want to win, so...fingers crossed!"

On the other side of the park, Mlle. Patisserie mutters to Edgar and Toulouse, "That Lana women better have been telling the truth about those cherries."

She threatens, coldly, "If I don't win, I will find her and her *master* and make them eat their words, which won't be nearly as tasty as some pastry."

"Ladies and gentlemen," a voice proclaims through the loudspeaker.

"The Bakerstown Baking Competition judging is about the begin. Competitors, please make your way to the gazebo."

The voice is that of Mayor Kevin Dimarchos. Every year, the Bakerstown mayor serves as emcee of the competition. It's really is a big deal.

Each baker moves to the table at center of the park and stands nervously behind their entry in order of tasting. The order goes: Mr. Roggen, Mlle. Patisserie, Ms. Pennybottom, Mrs. Biscotto, and so on.

The judges are a who's-who of the baking world. Professor Kolach of the Cuisson Institute is the head judge. The executive pastry chef of the exclusive Grape Vine Inn restaurant in the capital city of Haut, John Deda, and the famous celebrity pasta chef, Josephine Nonna, round out the panel of judges.

"Not too dry. The raisins add a nice sweetness and are still quite plump. This would be wonderful with a cup of tea and honey," Chef Deda says of Mr. Roggen's pumpernickel.

"I agree," Chef Kolach says. "Very good, Mr. Roggen. Thank you."

"Judges, next you have Mlle. Patisserie with her cherry tartlet," Mayor Dimarchos says.

Chef Nonna takes a bite of the cursed tartlet.

"Absolutely amazing!" she says, enthusiastically.

"By far the best thing I've ever tasted!" Chef Deda agrees.

Mlle. Patisserie is smiling broadly. "This might actually be working," she thinks to herself.

Chef Kolach looks intensely at the tartlet. He takes a second bite. Mlle. Patisserie's eyes are wide as she waits for his opinion.

Finally, he says, "Well done, Charlotte. Very well done. This tartlet is simply perfect."

Mlle. Patisserie can see victory in her grasp.

Miles above them, at the top of Mount Jadu, Bruxa Mala and her sister Juniper are watching the events unfold in their crystal ball. Bruxa Mala grins.

At the other side of the diamond table, for the first time in a thousand years, Juniper is worried for the Balance.

Back in Bakerstown..."Now, our reigning champion, Abigail Pennybottom and her entry, Rosie Raspberry Sensation cupcakes. Judges, please try the cupcakes," the Mayor directs.

"Disgusting!" Chef Nonna says as she spits out Ms. Pennybottom's cupcake into a napkin.

"Horrible! Not worth feeding to pigs!" Chef Deda exclaims.

"Abigail, I would have expected better from you," Chef Kolach says, disappointedly.

Ms. Pennybottom is crushed. She was fine with losing, but not like this. She never expected her cupcakes were *disgusting* or *horrible*. Hector, Napoleon, and the rest of the crowd are shocked.

Mlle. Patisserie smiles an even bigger smile and the judges continue the tasting.

"Ugh!"

"No! Terrible!"

"You call this a scone!?"

Mrs. Biscotto and the rest of the bakers don't fare any better than Ms. Pennybottom.

Shortly after the last entry is sampled, Mayor Dimarchos announces, "Ladies and Gentlemen! The judges have come to a unanimous decision."

Mlle. Patisserie holds her breath in anticipation. Ms. Pennybottom just stares at her cupcake wondering what went wrong.

"The winner of this year's Bakerstown Baking Competition is...Charlotte Patisserie! Congratulations! Come up and get your prize!" the Mayor Proclaims.

"Thank you! Thank you! I always knew I was the best baker in Bakerstown!" Mlle. Patisserie brags.

"Your tartlet was superb," Chef Kolach says. "What was your secret?"

Mlle. Patisserie mischievously replies, "I just have the best cherries around."

"It is my pleasure to present to you the blue ribbon of first place in the Bakerstown Baking Competition for your cherry tartlet," Mayor Dimarchos says as he awards Mlle. Patisserie her blue ribbon.

Just as Mlle. Patisserie's fingers touch the prize, clouds fill the sky and a peal of thunder shakes the air. It's not such a nice day in Bakerstown, anymore.

• • • • •

CASTLE DOIS RIGHT AFTER THE BAKING COMPETITION

DAY 1 OF THE TIPPING

"Sister, what have you done?" Juniper rises from her from her gold chair and asks Bruxa Mala with concern.

"I've waited a thousand years for this day, my dear Juniper," Bruxa Mala states, triumphantly, settling deeper into her onyx seat.

"By the end of this week, the Balance will be no more. Darkness will rule the world!" she promises. As she watches Mlle. Patisserie raise the blue ribbon in victory, she laughs an evil laugh.

6

Something Rosie Happens...

"I can't believe it," Ms. Pennybottom says sadly to Napoleon. They're seated in the living room of Hector's house.

Napoleon, jumps off the arm of the sofa and climbs up Ms. Pennybottom's arm to nuzzle her neck in an effort to comfort his best friend. She snuggles him back warmly, thankful for the little mouse.

Hector walks into the living room with a tray of tea and cookies, saying, "I'm so sorry, Abby. I can't believe you lost like that. I tried one of your cupcakes. They were delicious."

Ms. Pennybottom says nothing as she slowly shakes her head.

"I have no idea what got into those judges," Hector goes on, confused. "I just don't get it."

Suddenly, a pure bright light flashes, and two women appear in Hector's living room, one with shining, golden hair and sky-blue eyes, the other with a kind smile and a mane of platinum blond hair.

"Worry not, my dear Abigail," the golden-haired woman said, comfortingly. "You did nothing wrong."

Stunned by the sudden appearance of two women from out of thin air, Ms. Pennybottom, Hector, and Napoleon look to one another confused and more than a little frightened.

· · · · ·

Not too far away, Mlle. Patisserie twirls around her house in delight at finally beating Ms. Pennybottom.

"For two decades I've tried to beat Abigail, little Miss Perfect," she says with a sneer. "Finally, I've done it!"

Slowly, an inky black spot grows out of the shadows in the corner of her sitting room. Distracted by her ill-gotten glee, Mlle. Patisserie doesn't notice the spot or the two shapes that emerge from the gloom: a woman with onyx black hair and cruel, violet eyes and Lana, whom Mlle. Patisserie already knows.

"I told you the cherries would work," Lana says.

Mlle. Patisserie jumps in fright at the sudden comment, nearly hitting the ceiling, but she recovers her cool quickly and says, jabbing a finger toward the other woman, "I'm guessing this is your mysterious master."

"This is Bruxa Mala, Keeper of the Dark, sorceress of dark magic and the enchanter of your cherries. It is she that *allowed* you to beat Pennybottom," Lana explains, drawing out the word "allowed".

"Well, I guess I should thank you, then." Mlle. Patisserie says.

"Yes, you should. And, that isn't a *thank you*," Bruxa Mala snarls.

Mlle. Patisserie feels a wave of cold terror wash over her when she looks into the cruel, frozen eyes of Bruxa Mala.

She manages to eke out, "Th-th-thank you."

"You're welcome," Bruxa Mala replies, arrogantly.

"Now sit down," she orders. "Your work is far from finished. You may have beaten your old friend, but now you must destroy her."

• • • • •

"Where did you come from?" Hector asks the mysterious figures that are standing in his living room.

"Who are you?" adds Ms. Pennybottom.

"Squeeeeaaaak squeak squeeeak?" questions Napoleon.

I believe the miniscule mouse was asking, "What in the name of cheddar is going on?!?"

"Friends, do not be afraid," assures the golden-haired woman. "My name is Juniper. I am the Keeper of the Light and a sorceress of light magic."

She points to the woman next to her.

"This is Nata, my apprentice."

At her introduction, Nata bows a small bow.

"We have been watching you and your old friend Charlotte Patisserie these past few days," Juniper explains.

"Watching us... what are you talking about?" Ms. Pennybottom asks.

"That is a long story," Nata says with a sigh.

"One that I shall tell you," Juniper adds. "For this is a very important tale, indeed. It is a story one thousand years in the making. The ending, however, has not yet been written. How it ends will decide the fate of the world for the next thousand years."

She looks at Ms. Pennybottom and says, "And, you, Abigail, play a starring role."

Juniper tells Ms. Pennybottom, Napoleon and Hector the tale of the previous two Keepers of

Magic and her sister's betrayal a thousand years ago. She explains the importance of Bakerstown, the Balance, the Equalis, and the Tipping. Lastly, she tells Ms. Pennybottom all about the enchanted cherries and Mms. Patisserie's sneaky win at the baking competition.

She ends her story by saying,

"My sister is trying to destroy the Balance. That is why she gave the cursed cherries to Patisserie. She seeks to turn the people of Bakerstown to the Dark."

Hector and Napoleon are dumbstruck at Juniper's saga. Despite the shocking story, Ms. Pennybottom is relieved slightly to hear that her cupcakes weren't so terrible after all. She knew they were tasty, and, for some reason, magic and sorceresses make more sense to her than her cupcakes being gross.

She asks, "What could a baking competition possibly have to do with the end of the world?"

"The baking competition was just the beginning," Juniper explains.

"Charlotte Patisserie was already moving toward the Dark on her own. It was an easy matter for my sister to nudge her the rest of the way. The cursed cherries were just the push she needed. Accepting them broke her balance and made her one with the Dark."

Juniper continues, "A shadowy circle, with Mlle. Patisserie at its center will grow, swallowing person after person, until the whole of Bakerstown loses its Balance, unless you stop it."

"Me?" Ms. Pennybottom asks, feeling confused and very overwhelmed.

"Yes," Juniper answers, "The rules of magic prevent me from acting directly against my sister. I can only provide assistance."

Juniper looks deeply at Ms. Pennybottom and says, "You are good, Abigail, truly good. You must be a guide for the Essence of Light. As such, you are Guardian of the Light."

"Wait. Guardian? Guide? Essence of Light? What is happening?" Hector questions, nearly lost.

"I'm no guardian or guide. I'm just a baker" Ms. Pennybottom says. "Besides, how can I guide something I've never heard of?"

Juniper instructs Ms. Pennybottom, "Go into the kitchen and pick up your last Rosie Raspberry Sensation cupcake."

"Okay. If you say so," Ms. Pennybottom says as she cautiously walks into the kitchen, puzzled by the sudden change of topics.

She reaches out to grab the last cupcake off of the kitchen counter. But, instead of feeling cake and frosting between her finger tips, she feels a small hand grab hers.

Startled, Ms. Pennybottom jumps and screams, "Ahhh!"

"Don't be scared. I'm really nice," a sweet voice replies.

Ms. Pennybottom blinks a few times and sees a girl, about ten years old with wavy strands of rosy pink and lemony yellow hair, blue eyes and a bright, big smile sitting on the counter, where just a minute ago there was a raspberry-lemon cupcake.

"Abigail, meet the Essence of Light," Nata shouts from the other room. "Although, that name won't do at all. Bit of a mouthful, I'd say." You could almost hear her smiling.

At this, Napoleon faints and falls into Hector's lap. Hector nearly faints, too. Afraid of squishing his teeny friend, he manages to stay vertical.

Juniper clarifies what's happening to the group, "Ms. Pennybottom, you made your cupcakes out of love...a love of baking and a love of making people happy. As such, they are made of Light."

She goes on, "I was able to take that love and that Light and make a someone of pure goodness. She is the Essence of Light. She will be our warrior against the Dark. You must guide her in the battles to come."

"How will I know what to do?" Ms. Pennybottom asks, more than a little overwhelmed at what she's being asked to do.

"When the time comes, you will know. Until then, you and this young lady should get acquainted," Juniper answers, cryptically.

"And, figure out a better name than *Essence of Light*, too," adds Nata.

Another blinding flash of light, and Juniper and her assistant are gone.

"Um, Hello," Ms. Pennybottom says to the girl. "My name is Abigail."

"Hi!" the girl replies. "I don't really have a name."

"Yes, so I understand. Well, we're going to change that right now," Ms. Pennybottom promises.

She muses, "Let's see. You used to be a cupcake."

Ms. Pennybottom can't quite believe she's trying to name a magical girl who appeared on her kitchen counter out of nowhere and who used to be a cupcake.

I can't really believe it either. It's too crazy to make up, even for a story. But, hey, it's been a weird day.

"Your hair looks exactly like the raspberry frosting I made for the cupcakes, and I made that frosting to match the rosiness of the petunias I grow in my garden," she explains. "Hmmmm..."

The girl hops off the counter and exclaims happily, "I love it! It's perfect! My name is Rosie Petunia! Pleased to meet you," she says holding out her hand, formally.

"Rosie Petunia?" Ms. Pennybottom asks. "Really?"

"I like it," Hector says. "It has a nice ring to it, and you have to admit, it does match her hair."

"What do you think, Napoleon?" Ms. Pennybottom wonders.

Still a little shocked at what just happened, Napoleon smiles and holds out his paw to shake Rosie's hand.

"Okay then," Ms. Pennybottom says. "I guess that makes it official."

"Rosie Petunia it is. Please to make your acquaintance," she says as she shakes Rosie's hand.

"Let's go home," she says, still a little shaky at the whole situation. "I think we have a lot to talk about."

• • • • •

Bruxa Mala has just finished telling Mlle. Patisserie the same story that Juniper told Ms. Pennybottom and her friends.

Edgar and Toulouse are hiding under the coffee table, absolutely terrified at the evil women in their home.

"There are rules to magic," Bruxa Mala tells Mlle. Patisserie. "I'm not allowed to fight my sister or the Light directly. I need... *tools*."

She looks Mlle. Patisserie up and down and says, "You're one of my tools."

Mlle. Patisserie is offended at being called a tool, but is smart enough to say quiet.

Lana laughs to herself.

"I used you to make your cherry tartlet," Bruxa Mala explains.

"What use is a cherry tartlet in all this?" Mlle. Patisserie questions.

"If you'd be quiet, she'll tell you," Lana says.

Mlle. Patisserie turns her gaze to the floor.

"Baking is special to my sister and me. Baking is even how we became the Keepers of Magic. You see, I needed you to bake something completely dark. You had to bake something for the sole purpose of making someone miserable. Something totally selfish. You did that. Your cherry tartlet broke your Balance, making you mine."

Mlle. Patisserie thinks back to her first meeting with Lana. "*No catch*! Yeah right!" she says silently to herself.

"Your tartlet is a thing of the Dark. It will become the Essence of Dark, my soldier in the battle against the Light," Bruxa Mala says. "It will be your job to watch over her as Guardian of the Dark"

"Her? It's just a pastr-" Mlle. Patisserie starts.

"SILENCE!" Bruxa Mala screams.

Turning toward dining table and the lone cherry tartlet, she says, "Wake up, Cereza."

Magically, a girl with cherry red hair and dark brown eyes materializes where the tartlet used to be.

"I'm here, master," Cereza utters in a menacing whisper.

"Excellent," Bruxa Mala says. "Tool, this girl is the Essence of Dark. Watch over her. If she fails in her battles, I will blame you."

There's a sensation of falling in the room as all light is sucked away. When the feeling is gone, so are Bruxa Mala and Lana, leaving only Mlle. Patisserie, Cereza, and a terrified Edgar and Toulouse.

7

The Battle Begins, but First, Jewelry...

"Good morning, Rosie," Ms. Pennybottom says, entering her kitchen.

She still can't quite believe what happened the night before, but the sight of a girl with pink and yellow hair making pancakes in her kitchen is enough to push away any leftover doubt.

"Hi, Abby!" Rosie replies cheerfully. "I'm making blueberry pancakes. Want some?"

Not sure how a ten-hour old person knows how to make pancakes all by herself, Ms. Pennybottom chalks it all up to magic and answers, "I'd love some," and sets about making a very, very, very, very strong pot of coffee.

Napoleon wakes up to the rattling of coffee cups. Throwing off the miniature blankets from his teeny dollhouse bed in the corner to the kitchen counter, he rubs the sleep from his eyes and looks around for a breakfast of his own. Not wanting to wait for the pancakes, he steals a particularly large blueberry and gets to chowing down.

The mouse appears to have fully recovered from the previous night's mysterious and amazing events, since he doesn't seem bothered at all that Rosie is there. Mice are resilient like that. We can learn a lot from mice.

Pulling the last fluffy pancake off the pan, Rosie, Napoleon and Ms. Pennybottom sit at the kitchen table to enjoy their breakfast... well, second-breakfast for Napoleon.

"These are really great, Rosie," Ms. Pennybottom says.

"Thanks Abby!" Rosie answers. "I'm really happy you like them."

As you know, Ms. Pennybottom isn't a mouse; so, she hasn't fully recovered from the mysterious and amazing events of the night before. But, having a resiliency all her own, she manages, between bites of some of the best pancakes she's ever tasted, to ask Rosie, "What do you know about why you're here? Do you know what you're supposed to do?"

Thinking carefully about her answer, Rosie looks down at her empty plate then out at the sky — which is oddly split in half. One side is sunny without a single cloud, and the other half is a foreboding gray, filled with clouds and mist. She finally answers, "I'm not sure, but I think I'll know what I need to do when I need to do it."

"I guess I understand, but that's not too helpful. I'm supposed to guide you, but I'm not sure how," Ms. Pennybottom says, unsure. "I guess we'll both have to figure it out as we go along."

"Sounds like a good plan," Rosie says cheerfully. "I don't remember anything before you grabbed my hand in the kitchen last night, but I know how to talk, how to walk and how to make pancakes. I'm not sure how I know. I just do."

She shrugs her small shoulders and continues, "I think we'll just know what to do when the time is right."

She smiles at Ms. Pennybottom as she gently pets a pancake-stuffed Napoleon, who promptly burps in satisfaction. "I am made of magic, after all," she says with a laugh and knowing smile.

Ms. Pennybottom decides to accept the mysterious girl's answer and see what happens. Setting aside her pending role in saving the world, she changes topics to something a bit closer to normal and asks, "What do you want to do today?"

"I dunno," Rosie answers.

"Well," Ms. Pennybottom says, "I closed my bakery for a few days so I could get ready for the competition and bake the cupca... err... you, I guess."

"That'll never not be weird," Ms. Pennybottom confesses before continuing, "Since we don't have any battles to go fight right yet, I should probably get back to work. Wanna come?"

"That sounds like so much fun!" Rosie yells gleefully. "Can I help bake?"

"After those pancakes, absolutely!" Ms. Pennybottom promises.

· · · · ·

Across town in another kitchen that isn't nearly so cozy, Mlle. Patisserie takes a small sip of her steaming coffee.

"Okay. You're here," she says to Cereza. "Now what?"

"Now we turn Bakerstown to the Dark. Duh," Cereza replies, not looking up from her breakfast of orange scones and cream. Like Rosie and her pancakes, Cereza baked the scones, herself. Unlike Rosie, she didn't save any for Mlle. Patisserie.

"And, what, exactly does that mean?" Mlle. Patisserie asks, irked at the bratty girl.

Huffing in annoyance, Cereza explains, with the slightest bit more detail, "It means I go around and make people do bad things and be mean to each other."

"Be mean to each other?" Mlle. Patisserie asks for clarification. Getting only a blank stare in reply, Mlle. Patisserie realizes she's unlikely to get anything else from the sullen creature that's sitting at her table. She sighs and says, "Fine. I have to go to work. What are you going to do?"

"Where's your TV?" Cereza asks, looking around and not seeing one.

"I don't have one," Patisserie answers. A small smirk of satisfaction crosses her lips as she sees Cereza's annoyance at that answer.

"Then what am I supposed to do all day?" Cereza challenges.

"I'm sure you're perfectly capable of occupying yourself. Don't you have bad things to do?" Mlle. Patisserie goads.

"It's not like I have a to-do list. Don't you know anything?" Cereza says snidely.

"Fine," Mlle. Patisserie says, turning away. "If you want, you can come with me."

Mlle. Patisserie could almost hear Cereza's eyes roll as the evil girl answers.

Realizing she'd be very bored all day with nothing to do, Cereza decides, "Ugh! I guess I'll go with you."

• • • • •

You already know that Ms. Pennybottom and Mlle. Patisserie are both bakers, but did you know that their bakeries are across the street from each other? I'm guessing not, unless you've been to Bakerstown.

Ms. Pennybottom's bakery is called *Flour & Sugar?* It's the most popular bakery in town, or at least it was. Ever since she opened her shop, every day, the townspeople of Bakerstown would line up for her fresh-baked delights.

This morning, just like every morning, Ms. Pennybottom is hard at work making bread and cookies and cakes and pies and donuts and lots of other stuff to sell to the hungry Bakerstown customers. Only today, Rosie is helping.

The chef and her magical assistant make quick work of filling the shelves with fresh, delicious inventory for a day full of hungry customers.

Oddly, the morning passes with only one customer, Hector. It's not odd that Hector came in to the shop. He comes in every morning and orders a toasted everything bagel with veggie cream cheese and a hot cocoa with whipped cream. It's odd that he's the first and only customer of the day, though. Ms. Pennybottom is rather worried and wondering why no one else has come into her bakery, not even her other regulars.

· · · · ·

Earlier that morning, when Mlle. Patisserie was assembling the first dough of the day, Cereza asked, "You kicked Pennybottom's bottom at the baking competition, thanks to me; so, how are you gonna kick her butt today?"

The little brat had a point. Suddenly realizing she hadn't thought that far ahead, Mlle. Patisserie's was only able to respond with, "Ughhhh..."

"Yeah. I thought so," Cereza said. "Leave it to me."

As a result of Cereza's cruel imagination, at opening time, the front window of Mlle. Patisserie's bakery has a big red sign that reads,

> Why go the bakery with the worst pastry the Bakerstown judges have ever tasted, when you can buy the best? Say 'Pennybottom is the worst' and get 15% off your order.

The sign must have worked because by ten in the morning, Mlle. Patisserie's bake shop, *In It for the Dough*, has a huge line that wraps around the block.

Inside, Edgar and Toulouse look on in amazement as Mlle. Patisserie giddily sells pastry after pastry to hungry customers — more than she's ever sold before.

• • • • •

Meanwhile across the street, Ms. Pennybottom sees *In It for the Dough's* gigantic line.

Disheartened, she looks at Napoleon and Rosie and says, "I don't understand. These are my friends. They've been coming here every day for years. What happened?"

Gazing through her front window, Ms. Pennybottom sees the next person in line to pay in Mlle. Patisserie's shop is a kind looking man with messy brown hair and dark green overalls. His name is Otto Mechaniker and owns the car repair garage.

"Look, there's Otto. We've been friends forever," she says to no one in particular. "He comes in every morning for a brötchen and honig for breakfast before he starts his day. Why isn't he coming over?"

Rosie looks up at her friend. She can feel Abby's sadness. Instinctively, Rosie knows it's not right. Immediately, she turns, leaves *Sugar & Flower* and runs across the street. She approaches Otto, taps on his arm and asks, "Excuse me, sir. Can I ask why you're getting your breakfast here today?"

Before he has a chance to answer, Mlle. Patisserie shouts, "Next!"

Otto approaches the counter and says, "Pennybottom is the worst! I get fifteen-percent off, right?" He's the first person to say the words from Cereza's sign.

"Why of course," Mlle. Patisserie answers with a malicious smile.

Satisfied at his breakfast and his discount, Otto ignores Rosie's question and leaves the bakery. He doesn't ever so much as glance at Ms. Pennybottom across the street.

At that exact moment, the sky outside gets a little darker and there's a loud crack of thunder.

• • • • •

Just as the sound of thunder starts to fade, Cereza looks down at a necklace she's wearing. It's a gold chain with a small charm in the shape of a heart. Earlier, the charm was half clear, like a diamond on top, and half dark, like onyx on the bottom. She'd noticed it earlier, but thought it was only a part of the outfit she'd appeared wearing.

But, just as that man wearing the ugly green outfit betrayed his friend for a small discount on some rolls and honey, the charm glowed a bright light. As the flash of light fades, Cereza notices it now looks like the onyx part is a bit bigger, having taking over some of the diamond half.

Cereza now understands exactly what she is supposed to do.

• • • • •

Rosie stands there, amazed at what she'd just heard Otto say about one of his oldest friends, Abigail Pennybottom, when she hears a peal of thunder. She looks down at a bright light coming from her own heart-shaped pendant which is a near twin to Cereza's, only Rosie's pendant is half diamond on bottom and half onyx at the top. Or, at least it was.

Once the light fades, Rosie notices that the diamond half is smaller, having been eaten away by the onyx.

Suddenly understanding why she appeared in Bakerstown, the meaning of Juniper's words and what she is meant to do, Rosie looks up to see another girl staring at her own crystal pendant on the other side of the bakery. This other girl, Cereza, could be her twin, apart from her hair, of course.

· · · · ·

Rosie Petunia and Cereza lock eyes across the shop. Despite never having met before, the two magical girls instantly recognize each other and instinctively know they're not the only ones battling for the heart of Bakerstown.

Rosie turns and runs from Mlle. Patisserie's bakery. Cereza sets off after her.

Rosie stops in the middle of the street between the rival bakeries and turns to face Cereza. Cereza stops inches from Rosie. The two magical girls stare deeply into each other's eyes as if trying to understand all they could about their foe.

"My name is Cereza. Remember it," Cereza says, flatly.

"I'm Rosie Petunia, and Light will always win," Rosie declares.

"I'm afraid you won't win," Cereza snarls. "The people of Bakerstown belong to the Dark."

"Not yet," Rosie answers. "There's good in all of them, and I'll prove it to you."

• • • • •

CASTLE DOIS, MORNING, DAY 2 OF THE TIPPING

Deep inside Castle Dois, a light shines from a heart-shaped pendant resting on her chest as Juniper, the Keeper of the Light falls to one knee in agony. Nata rushes to her friend's side and helps her up.

"It's started," Juniper says. "The first heart has taken a side, and they have turned Dark. The fate of everyone is up to Rosie and Abigail now."

· · · · ·

Bruxa Mala lets out a loud and deep laugh as an onyx and diamond heart-shaped pendant hanging from a gold chain suddenly glows as the onyx half grows just a bit.

"So, it begins," the Keeper of the Dark says, clutching her charm.

"Master, does that mean the plan in working?" Lana asks.

"Of course, it means the plan is working, you fool!" the Keeper of the Dark snarls at her minion.

"Cereza is doing exactly as I'd hoped. One by one, she's turning the hearts of Bakerstown to the Dark. As soon as half of the population of Bakerstown plus one solitary heart turns dark, we will have swayed the Tipping and brought darkness to the entire world."

Bruxa Mala walks over to the golden stand and the book resting upon it. She says to her apprentice,

"The last chapter of this book is blank. Do you know why?"

"B-b-because you haven't written it?" Lana answers sheepishly.

"Have you learned nothing!?!" Bruxa Mala shouts. "I didn't write the book. This is *The Book of Balance*. It tells the story of the Balance throughout time."

Afraid to ask any more questions, Lana just looks at her master, hoping she would continue.

Luckily for Lana, she does.

"The tale of the first two Keepers, Scura and Lux, how they came upon the hearts in pendants my sister and I wear, the fate of every Tipping, the name of every Keeper of the Light and of the Dark, the origin every Essence of Light and Essence of Dark... all of it. *The Book of Balance* tells all of our stories. It told the previous Keepers when my sister and I would encounter the willow tree and how I would lose my balance to the Dark. It told how Pennybottom and Patisserie would become the Guardians and how their hearts would create the Cereza and that other one."

"Rosie Petunia," Lana offers.

"I know her name!" Bruxa chides. Leafing through the book, Bruxa comes upon a blank page.

"The book. It stops here. After Cereza and Rosie are born, there's nothing else. For the first time in thousands upon thousands of years, the fate of the Tipping is not predestined. We don't know what's going to happen."

· · · · ·

"What does that mean?" Nata ask Juniper, who has just told her the exact same tale as Bruxa told Lana on the other side of the castle.

"My dear apprentice," Juniper explains. "It means that this is the final Tipping. Whichever side is victorious decides the fate of the world, forever.

"How can we trust the fate of the world to two small girls who were pastries only a day ago?" Nata asks. It a logical question, really.

Juniper smiles at her friend in response. "Don't worry. Rosie will find her way. She has something Cereza will never have."

• • • • •

MOUNT JADU, MORNING, DAY 2 OF THE TIPPING

Deep in the woods of Mount Jadu, inside a cave lit by a single candle, three dogs are curled around each other sleeping, as they have been for a thousand years. The moment the first heart chooses a side, they awaken. In a heartbeat, all three run out of the cave toward Bakerstown.

8

A Three Dog Night...

"A whole day and only one customer," Ms. Pennybottom says quietly as she sits in her parlor and stares into a cup of green tea with honey. "Only Hector came in all day."

"It's Cereza. It's all her fault," Rosie says.

Earlier in the day, Rosie told Ms. Pennybottom of her confrontation with Cereza and what happened with her necklace.

"Oh, Rosie, what are we going to do?" Ms. Pennybottom asks.

. . . . .

As soon as the words leave her lips a strange whining comes from outside, along with a scratching at the door. Instantly, Napoleon is on guard, grabbing a small plastic sword and swinging it about.

"Calm down, my little friend, it's probably just the neighbor's dog hoping for some leftover scraps," Ms. Pennybottom explains as she moves to open the door.

Outside are three small dogs, each barely bigger than a large mixing bowl. One is powerful and lean with intelligent eyes. A sense of strength and security wafts off of her like the aroma of apples from a pie fresh from the oven.

Next to her is graceful and lithe dog with a happy, joyful look in her eyes and a wildly wagging tail. Something about her just makes you smile as she seems to understand what it takes to live your best life.

The third dog is playful yet wise. From her little belly, you can tell she enjoys life and from the look in her eyes you can tell she's very smart, too. She'd definitely give Napoleon a run for his money in the snacking category.

There's a tremendous feeling of power and loyalty coming from all three animals standing before Ms. Pennybottom. Plus, well...they're really adorable.

Suddenly, the first pup speaks. Well, it doesn't so much speak as Rosie, Napoleon and Ms. Pennybottom magically understand what she's thinking. Napoleon sets down his plastic sword.

"We are the *Three Dogs of Truth*. I am Domina, the Strong. This," looking at the second dog, "is Anatra, the Vibrant. And, lastly, I present Lila the Wise. We keep the story of Light and Dark and guard the Cave and its flame."

"Where did you come from?" Rosie asks the three pups.

Anatra answers, "We've been asleep for the past thousand years. The first choosing woke us from our nap."

"The Dark has taken their first heart, and the battle has begun," Lila adds.

"Why are you here? What do you want?" Ms. Pennybottom asks, scared of what the answer might be.

Looking at Rosie and Ms. Pennybottom, Domina explains, "The Keeper of the Light came to you, the Essence of Light, and you, her guide, to tell you of the Balance, the Equalis and the Tipping. What she did not tell you is how the battle will be won and what happens after."

She continues, "As you know, Bakerstown is split evenly in two by the Equalis. Normally, just like every other person in the world, the hearts of all those in Bakerstown are balanced between Light and Dark. However, during the Tipping, those same hearts become vulnerable. They can be pushed to one side or the other, breaking the balance."

Anatra takes over telling the story, saying, "At the end of the tipping, in five days' time, it's your job, Rosie Petunia, to ensure that fifty-percent of the people of Bakerstown plus one heart choose the Light. Your opposite, Cereza, the Essence of Dark, will be working her hardest to tip the scale to Darkness."

Lila closes the tale, "Your pendent, when it glowed... a heart was turned to the Dark."

"Otto," Ms. Pennybottom whispers.

"Yes," Lila answers.

The small dog continues, "Every time a heart is turned, the ratio of diamond and onyx of your pendant will change, keeping track of each heart. If your pendant becomes completely onyx, the Dark will have won."

All three dogs step closer to Rosie. Anatra explains, "This is the tenth Tipping. It is also the last, and you are the final in a long line of Essences of Light. Whichever side wins will learn the location of the Cave and secret to sealing the fate of humanity forever."

"I can't let that happen!" Rosie shouts with tears in her eyes, afraid of the task in front of her.

Ms. Pennybottom grabs Rosie's hand, tightly, and says, "We won't. We can do this together."

Domina finishes, "It is our role to ensure you and Cereza know what is at stake. When one side earns the final heart, we will return to guide them to the Cave. Until then, we will remain at our post."

Having told their tale and completed their task, the Three Dogs of Truth — Domina, Anatra and Lila — turn and walk away into the night.

• • • • •

Mlle. Patisserie is sitting in her living room, counting the profits from the most successful day she's had since opening her bakery. Cereza is in the other room terrorizing Toulouse, when a now-familiar inky black pool spreads across the floor.

Mlle. Patisserie jumps, slightly, at the sight, then thinks to herself, "I should really be used to this by now."

Sensing the arriving darkness, Cereza walks calmly into the room.

"You did well today, my child," Bruxa Mala says to Cereza. The small girl only smiles a cruel smile in response.

"She did well?" Mlle. Patisserie questions. "I'm the one who destroyed Pennybottom today."

"You?" the Keeper of the Dark snarls. "You did nothing. Cereza made the sign that skyrocketed your profits. She is the one to turn the people of Bakerstown against their beloved Abigail Pennybottom."

Cereza sticks her tongue out at Patisserie then says, "When that man spoke against his friend, something happened. My necklace glowed and became more black."

"Exactly, my dear. You broke his balance and his heart turned Dark."

There's a scratching at the front door.

"Ah, right on time," Bruxa Mala says as she opens the door, revealing three dogs.

"Greetings. We are the Three Dogs of Truth."

• • • • •

"I'm ready," Cereza says.

"I know you are. Do not disappoint me, either of you," Bruxa Mala says, dripping with malice, responding to

Cereza but staring at Mlle. Patisserie.

9

Heart for Heart...

BAKERSTOWN, MORNING, DAY 3 OF THE TIPPING

By the next morning, word of the rise in popularity of *In It for the Dough* had spread all around town. When you live in a village as small as Bakerstown, no news stays private for long. For a second morning in row, the line to get into Mlle. Patisserie's bakery winds around the block.

Mlle. Patisserie is absolutely thrilled in her new-found popularity — and, not just because she was selling out of all of baked goods. Her cruel streak ran so deep that she felt more joy in the misery her rival, Ms. Pennybottom, was feeling.

Looking out the front window of her own bakery, Ms. Pennybottom frowns at the line for *In It for the Dough*. Her eyes meet Mlle. Patisserie's, just for a second, and Mlle. Patisserie smiles the meanest grin. Ms. Pennybottom's heart turns to lead in her chest.

She quickly looks away, finding Napoleon sitting on Rosie's shoulder just in time to see Rosie's pendant glow brightly. Once the light dims, everyone sees that the onyx has eaten away at a bit more of the diamond. Another heart had just turned dark — no doubt another former friend saying "Pennybottom is the worst!" for a small discount on a sugar cookie or lemon-poppy seed muffin across the street.

"If I didn't know what she's done and who she's working with, I'd be happy for Charlotte's success," Ms. Pennybottom laments to her friends.

"But," she continues, "She's trying to hurt the people of Bakerstown, the people I care about."

"Squeeeak," Napoleon says to console her friend. That means, "It's okay. We love you, and we'll do everything we can to defeat the Dark." Mouse language is a lot more efficient than English. They can pack a lot more words into one "squeak".

Rosie agrees, "That's right, Napoleon. We're go— "

Just then, Rosie was interrupted by the bell above the bakery's front door jingling.

All three of them turn toward the sound to see Lindsay Publizist, star reporter of the *Bakerstown Times Gazette*, walk through the door.

Before Lindsay found her love of journalism and her talent for digging out the truth from any story, she, Ms. Pennybottom and Mlle. Patisserie went to high school together and had been close friends. While the two bakers worked hard in mastering their tasty craft in the form of gooey brownies and flaky palmiers, Lindsay covered every Bakerstown Lion football game, chess tournament and student council election.

The three of them met when young Abby and Charlotte tied for first place in a district-wide cooking competition, bringing the blue-ribbon home to Bakerstown High. Lindsay was writing the story for the school paper, the *Lion Times*.

"Hey, Abby!" Lindsay effuses, cheerfully.

"Hi, Lindsay," says, brightening a bit at seeing her longtime friend.

"Not that I'm not happy to see you, but what brings you in?" Ms. Pennybottom asks.

"You didn't think a little thing like a bad bakeoff would keep me from my favorite blueberry pie, did you?" Lindsay asks, smiling from ear to ear.

Ms. Pennybottom smiles faintly at her friend's comment. She also knows her friend really well and recognizes when she's looking to get a scoop on a big story. She probes,

"I know that smile, Linds. What are you up to?"

"Fine," Lindsay answers. "The *Times Gazette* assigned me to cover the fallout from the baking competition. Everyone is talking about it."

"Don't remind me," Ms. Pennybottom says.

Lindsay explains, "It's not like that. I think there's more to the story than a bad batch of cupcakes. I've known you for a long time, and apart from your experimental anchovy-sourdough bread fiasco in college, I've never seen you to make anything bad...especially not that bad."

Ms. Pennybottom tilts her head and looks to her friend, waiting to hear more.

The reporter keeps going, "I'm going to find out the truth, and when I do, *Sugar & Flour* will be back in business."

Ms. Pennybottom, Napoleon and Rosie smile at that.

Since she's been a bit distracted by the story that's afoot, Lindsay didn't notice Rosie at first.

"Wait a minute," she shouts, staring at Rosie. "Who, the heck, are you?"

"I'm Rosie Petunia," Rosie answers, matter-of-factly. "I'm the Essence of Light."

Confused, Lindsay says, "The Essence of what, now?"

"Never mind," Ms. Pennybottom interjects. "It's a long story, and I promise to tell you everything later."

"Fine," the reporter mumbles reluctantly. "I'll hold you to that. Anyway...Now to the most important question...Where's my pie?" Lindsay asks.

Ms. Pennybottom happily chooses the best blueberry pie in the case and gives it to Lindsay. "Family and good friends discount," she says. "No charge."

Lindsay looks at her dear friend and says, "Abby, I know things are tough right now, but we'll get to the bottom of it. I promise."

With that, Lindsay thanked Ms. Pennybottom, took her pie and left the store. The moment the door closed, Rosie's heart amulet glowed bright enough to light the entire shop. For the first time, the onyx had shrunk. Lindsay Publizist was the first heart to choose the light.

Peering down at her necklace, Rosie breathed, "I have a plan."

• • • • •

MOUNT JADU, MORNING, DAY 2 OF THE TIPPING

The two Keepers sit across from each other, gazing into the crystal orb in the middle of their golden table. Both of their amulets flash brilliantly. Juniper's shines a bit more splendidly.

"It seems as if Rosie has begun to find her way," the Keeper of the Light breathes softly to her sister.

"Oh, shut up!" is her sister's only retort.

10

A Quiet Battle Rages...

BAKERSTOWN, FINAL DAYS OF THE TIPPING

Backstage of the Panya Theater, the young star of stage and screen, Sienna Stellateatro, is warming up for her latest audition. She is trying out for the lead role of "La Panettiera." As the highlight of this year's Bakerstown theatrical season, it's the most important role of her young career. Sienna's harshest rival, Aurora Ragazzaccia is auditioning for the same role.

Both actresses deliver auditions of a lifetime. Sienna captures the complex emotions of the star... her drive to be the best, her love of family. Aurora dives into the depths of desire to topple all in her path.

In the end, Sienna's stellar and authentic performance win out. The director, Direttore Dramma, chooses the rising star to headline their newest production. Sienna's honesty and genuine portrayal of the heroine are enough to sway the veteran director. Aurora is chosen as the understudy.

Cereza is watching in the wings.

"That role should have been yours," Cereza tells Aurora, behind the scenes. "You were so much better than her. You deserve this. You should do whatever you need to make it yours."

Egged on by Cereza's words, Aurora cannot handle the defeat. She storms Sienna's dressing room.

"I am the star!" Aurora screams. "This role should be mine!"

Red-faced and snarling with anger, Aurora picks up a makeup tray and throws it at Sienna's head, trying to force the young star from the production. She misses and shatters Sienna's mirror, instead.

"Aurora, don't worry," Sienna tries to console her young rival. "You did great. I'm sure you'll get the next role."

"No!" Aurora screams. "You'll never beat me again, no matter what! I'll do anything I need to do to best you!"

With that, Aurora storms out of Sienna's dressing room, slamming the door behind her.

As the cracks spread across Sienna's mirror, Rosie and Cereza's amulets shine brilliantly. But, neither darkness nor light gain any ground. The goodness in Sienna's heart binds her to the Light; while the horrible envy of Aurora ties her to the Dark that Cereza and Bruxa Mala are fighting for. The Light and the Dark gain one heart each. The battle continues...

· · · · ·

The Bakerstown Baking Competition is a major tourist event for the small village. As I mentioned, if you were paying attention, this is the biggest event in the Bakerstown annual calendar. Every inn and hotel near the town fill up months in advance.

As the premiere pet-friendly bed and breakfast in the area, the Casita Perrita is no exception. The proprietors, Fernando and Maria Bienvenida do everything they can to make their guests feel at home. Their inn is known far and wide as the finest place to stay in the entire region. As a matter of fact, the Bakerstown Travelers Association, the BTA, has given Casa Perrita a five-star rating the past six years in a row. That's the top rating available, you know. They even give fresh baked pan de yucas from *Sugar & Flour* to every guest as they check in.

This year, one particular guest will do almost as much to try and get a free stay...even lie. A few days after the historic events of the Bakerstown Baking Competition, Vil Egoista and her husband Ladron approach the front desk of the Casa Perrita to check out.

"This is the worst place we've ever stayed," Vil says to Maria, who is on duty at the front desk. "The towels smelled bad. The sheets were wrinkled. And, the minibar was full of *generic* candy."

Maria responds, "I'm sorry ma'am. I assure you, we do the best we can to make everyone's stay as perfect as possible. We only stock the finest name-brand candy. We wash and press the linens every day."

"I don't care what you *say* you do!" Ladron adds. "This stay was terrible, and we want a refund."

Now, both Fernando and Maria double check every room before a guest checks in, and they know the Egiosta's room was up to their exacting standards.

Rosie is delivering the latest batch of pan de yuca to the bed and breakfast when she hears the commotion at the front desk.

"Excuse me," she says to Vil and Ladron. "I don't think you're being fair. Fernando and Maria work very, very hard to make everyone feel at home here."

"Shut up, you little brat!" Vil chides, staring daggers at Rosie.

"Yeah! Stay out of it, kid!" Ladron adds.

After a brief silence, Maria says, "It's okay Rosie. If any guest is truly unhappy, we'll do whatever we can to make it right."

Maria faces the Egoistas and says, "I'm sorry you found your stay unpleasant. We'll make up for it. How about a free night and dinner at our restaurant?"

"That's better," Vil answers.

As the rude couple turns away from the front desk, Rosie's heart-shaped pendant brightens yet again. Another tie. The kindness of the Beinevenidas grow the Light by two hearts while the Ladrons gain two for the Dark. The battle rages on...

• • • • •

Napoleon accompanies Rosie on the delivery to Casa Perrita. While his friend is busy with the happenings at the front desk, he notices a small bright red mouse near the far wall of the inn's lobby. She was dragging several packs of candy — the same candy that was supposed to be in the inn's minibars. She was also the most gorgeous mouse Napoleon had ever seen. He's smitten.

"Let's go, Napoleon." Rosie says. The diminutive mouse doesn't hear her. He's still rather distracted.

"Yooohooo! Naaaaapoleooon!" Rosie urges more insistently. "You there, little guy?"

Napoleon turns to look at Rosie and nods. After a moment, the two turn to leave the inn. Napoleon glances over his shoulder for one last look at the red mouse. Much to Napoleon's disappointment, she's disappeared. Rosie and Napoleon make their way back to Ms. Pennybottom's bakery, but Napoleon can't get the image of the other mouse out of his head.

• • • • •

The mysterious red mouse sprints through a hole in the wall of the Casa Perrita's lobby, scampering outside and down the street to Mlle. Patisserie's house where Cereza is waiting for her.

Only the day before, Cereza was walking past Casa Perrita's outdoor restaurant, plotting ways to turn people to her side when she saw a small red mouse stealing food from diners' plates. She was so sneaky, no one but Cereza noticed her. Cereza knew she'd found a kindred spirit and a new partner.

"Was he there?" Cereza asks the crimson mouse. She nods affirmatively.

Both Edgar and Toulouse stare at her thinking just how tasty the little mouse would be.

"Good," Cereza says, ignoring the hungry gazes of her two companions. "Keep an eye on him and make sure he's distracted when the time is right."

"Oh, and Jordi," the Essence of Dark adds, "I'm counting on you."

Jordi the mouse nods curtly and runs off.

· · · · ·

Thomas and Vicki Glas have lived in Bakerstown all of their lives. Thomas is the town watchmaker and Vicki owns the florist shop right next door to *In It for the Dough.* Today, they're in the Bakerstown Farmers Market doing some shopping. You can't beat the produce at the farmers market. It really is the best around.

Vicki makes some of the tastiest banana cream pie around and is on the hunt for some prime bananas. It's a bit late in the season for bananas, so there aren't many left at the fruit stand — just one perfect bunch, as a matter of fact.

She reaches out for the last of the ripe yellow fruit when a small red mouse runs across her hand. She yelps and jumps back.

Cereza is also at the market. She isn't shopping for fruit or vegetables as much as she's looking to cause trouble.

As soon as she sees Vicki reach for the bananas and suddenly jump away, thanks to her furry garnet rodent associate, she grabs the last of the fruit.

"Too slow!" she says mockingly as she runs from the fruit stand, bananas in hand, without paying. Jordi continues to run amok through the fruit, biting an apple here, stealing a strawberry there — generally being a nuisance.

Sefina Saua is also shopping for fruit to make her puligi coconut pudding when Jordi bites her hand.

"Ahhh!" Sefina screams. "Stupid mouse! That hurt!"

She yells at Tiago Fruta, the proprietor of the fruit stand, "There are mice running around your shop! I'll have you closed down for this!"

Shocked at the presence of the red mouse, Tiago says, meekly, "I'm so sorry. I've never seen a mouse here before."

Still looking for fruit replace the lost bananas, Thomas tries to calm the other customer.

"We've been shopping here for years and have never seen a mouse in the fruit," he says.

"I don't care! I'll see you shut down!" Sefina shouts as she shoves past Thomas and Vicki.

"Don't worry," Vicki says to Tiago. We'll make sure everyone knows the quality of your fruit.

"Thank you so much," Tiago says. He reaches behind the counter and pulls out a perfect bunch of bananas.

"I've been saving these, but please take them," He says.

"Thank you," Vicki says. "We'll be sure to bring you a slice of pie!"

At the far end of the market, Cereza and Jordi are sharing a stolen banana when Cereza's amulet shines after the encounter at the fruit stand. Three hearts, Thomas, Vicki and Tiago choose Light, while Sefina choses Dark. The diamond half of the pendant gains just a bit over the onyx.

· · · · ·

Watching from the rafters of the farmers market, Edgar and Toulouse see what Cereza is doing to the people of Bakerstown — the same people that have always given them scraps of bread or bowls of milk when they were hungry, before they were taken in by Mlle. Patisserie. They look at each other, unsure if they've chosen the right side of this fight.

· · · · ·

For the next few days, the back and forth continues. Every time the Light makes a little progress, the Dark closes the gap. By the evening of the seventh day, the battle is tied. Despite Rosie's, Ms. Pennybottom's and Napoleon's best efforts, Cereza and Mlle. Patisserie match them, heart for heart. Half of the people of Bakerstown have chosen the Light and have chosen the Dark. Only one heart remains undecided — that of Hector Pantalones.

11

The Final Heart...

BAKERSTOWN, NIGHT, THE LAST DAY OF THE TIPPING

The problem with battles to save the fate of the world is that time doesn't just stop. If you're a baker, a mechanic, a watchmaker, a florist, an innkeeper or a tailor, you still need to keep working if you want to keep your business afloat.

After leaving a wonderful dinner with Ms. Pennybottom of beef stew with carrots, peas and potatoes, along with a side for warm French bread, Hector is back at his shop attending to a pile of alterations he'd neglected thanks to the craziness of the past few days.

He's thinking fondly of the conversation he'd shared with Ms. Pennybottom and realizing how much he likes being with her; how comfortable they are together. As he's threading the needle of his sewing machine to hem a pair of plaid suit pants for one of his regular customers, he hears a quiet knock. A folded piece of paper slides under his front door.

Hector gets up from his bench and picks up the note. Unfolding it, he reads,

> *Dear Hector,*
>
> *After spending time with you, I've decided we're not a good match. The apron you gave me, the dinners...You're trying too hard. I think I can do better. Good luck, and goodbye.*
>
> *Yours truly,*
>
> *Abby*

Shocked and confused, Hector crumples the letter in his hands an runs out the door toward Ms. Pennybottom's house, tears in his eyes. He doesn't see the girl with cherry red hair hiding in the bushes at the front of his house.

• • • • •

It's late and Napoleon is fast asleep in his little bed after finishing nearly a whole carrot and potato all by himself. The dreaming mouse belches and rolls over. Rosie and Ms. Pennybottom are sitting in the living room trying to figure out why Hector's heart is still undecided. He'd been supporting Rosie from the start. He was there when she first appeared. But, for some reason, his heart still needs to choose a side.

Distracted by the problem at hand, Rosie and Ms. Pennybottom don't notice Edgar, Toulouse and Jordi pry open the kitchen window, prop it ajar with a wooden spoon and sneak in. All three invaders remember the order they were given by Cereza and Mlle. Patisserie.

"Sneak into Pennybottom's kitchen and get the apron that awful tailor made her. Bring it outside and drop it in the trash," Mlle. Patisserie commanded.

"If that annoying mouse spots you, Jordi, distract him long enough for Edgar and Toulouse to get away," Cereza added.

Toulouse slinks toward the hook where Ms. Pennybottom hangs her apron. He's able pull it up with his paws just enough for Edgar to grab snag it off of the hook with his beak. The raven flies back through the open window, hauling the apron. Toulouse follows.

As they're about to make their make their escape, the apron's ribbon knocks over a measuring cup that was sitting next to the sink. The sound of the tumbling cup was enough to wake Napoleon. The mouse bolts upright and unsheathes his trusty plastic sword from its place next to his bed, ready to defend his home. Jordi instantly realizes the threat Napoleon poses to their plan.

Edgar is already outside with the apron, perched on the tree branch near Ms. Pennybottom's kitchen window. Toulouse is jumping from counter to counter, making his escape. Jordi knows she has to give the cat time to get away. To distract the other mouse, she locks eyes with Napoleon. Napoleon remembers the red mouse from Casa Perrita.

Toulouse pounces closer and closer to Jordi's spot on the window sill. She sees her opportunity. Feigning fear at the cat, she squeals in false terror.

"Squuuuueeeaaaaaaaak!"

With Toulouse pouncing quickly toward her, it was easy to look scared.

Calling on a look very similar to genuine fear, Jordi locks eyes with Napoleon. Reaching out with her tiny paw, she begs him for rescue from the big black cat. Despite his own dread, the valiant Napoleon swings his sword with a flourish and charges toward Jordi and the approaching Toulouse.

The moment Napoleon reaches her spot on the window, Jordi dives outside and, in mid-jump, kicks away the spoon that was holding the window open and sends it crashing onto Napoleon, crushing him.

Smiling a cruel smile at the hurt Napoleon, Jordi runs off into the night. Edgar and Toulouse see the hurt, selfless, little, grey mouse and both feel very, very guilty. They were okay with their master winning a baking competition and making people be mean to each other, but no one was supposed to get hurt. They drop the apron in the garbage can as ordered and run off into the night, questioning what they should do next.

• • • • •

The sound of a slamming window startles Rosie and Ms. Pennybottom. Both rush to the kitchen to see what happened. Rosie notices Napoleon first. He's trapped under the window sash.

"Oh no! Napoleon!" Rosie screams.

Ms. Pennybottom gasps and rushes to open the window to free her dear, brave friend. What she sees terrifies her.

The heroic little mouse is unconscious and barely breathing. Carefully bundling him into a towel, Rosie and Ms. Pennybottom rush Napoleon through the back door, heading for Dr. Dyr, the veterinarian, hoping to save his life.

• • • • •

Hector approaches Ms. Pennybottom's front door and is about to knock when something catches his eye. Sitting there on top of the trash can, next to discarded carrot peels and apple cores is a swatch of pink fabric with green spots. He brushes away the refuse to find the apron he made for Ms. Pennybottom... the one she said she loved. His face flushes with sadness and his heart drops into his gut.

"How could she?" Hector breathes to himself. "I thought we had something together." He takes another look at the stained and rejected apron as his sadness turns to anger. He turns toward home, boiling at his supposed rejection.

• • • • •

Rosie and Cereza's heart-shaped amulets glow more brightly than ever before. Once the light dims enough to see, both pendants have turned completely onyx and are glowing a faint red. The last heart has chosen. Hector's heart has chosen. And, he has chosen the Dark.

• • • • •

CASTLE DOIS, NIGHT, THE LAST DAY OF THE TIPPING

Juniper screams in pain has her pendant flashes blood red. She falls to her knees. Nata rushes to her side.

"Are you okay? What's happened?" she asks her friend and mentor.

"It's done. We've lost. Bakerstown has chosen the Dark," Juniper whispers, weakly.

The Keeper of the Light and her apprentice can hear a loud, shrill laugh.

"You feel that, sister?" Bruxa Mala shouts as she slams through the door into Juniper's study.

"I've won and there's nothing else you can do!"

Lana smiles a truly evil smile at Nata. She doesn't need to say anything. The grim and pained expression on Juniper's face is enough.

• • • • •

MOUNT JADU, NIGHT, THE LAST DAY OF THE TIPPING

Sensing the final heart has chosen a side, the Three Dogs of Truth make their way into town to guide Cereza and Mlle. Patisserie to their prize.

12

A Flickering Candle...

BAKERSTOWN, ONE DAY AFTER THE TIPPING

Mlle. Patisserie sits uncomfortably on a chair in her living room, afraid to draw the attention of her malevolent houseguests. Cereza, on the other hand, is beaming proudly at the praise she's receiving from those same guests — so is the latest addition to their little crew, Jordi. (That evil mouse may be as red as a strawberry, but she's nowhere near as sweet, especially not after what she did to

Napoleon.) Edgar and Toulouse are hiding behind the sofa.

"Well done, Cereza," Bruxa Mala praises. "You've proven capable in your task and bested your adversary."

She turns to Jordi and says, "And, you, my fiendish little friend, are a mouse after my own heart."

"Thank you, master. Now what happens?" Cereza asks.

"Now we can snuff out the light, forever!" Lana answers.

"The Dogs should be here soon to answer that very question." Bruxa Mala answers, her smile fading a bit at the prospect of waiting.

• • • • •

Ms. Pennybottom and Rosie leave the veterinarian's office after dropping Napoleon off. The kindly doctor promised he would do all he could for their friend, but the gallant mouse was in bad shape. Still, there were few as hardy and as plucky as Napoleon.

They are both so worried and wish they could stay with Napoleon to offer whatever help they can. But, the moment Rosie's amulet turned completely black and began shinning red, they knew they had to leave Dr. Dyr to do his work. Hard as it is, they must set aside their fears for Napoleon and focus on preventing the Dark from taking over.

Time was up. Rosie and Ms. Pennybottom rush back home to figure what, if anything, they could do to stem the tide of darkness from sweeping over everything.

• • • • •

It's late and the party assembled in Mlle. Patisserie's living room is growing restless.

"It's time. Let us in," Lila says as the Three Dogs of Truth sit outside of Mlle. Patisserie's front door.

Cereza hurries to open the door.

"About time," Bruxa Mala scoffs as Domina, Anatra and Lila enter the house.

"It's best for you not to confuse us with your minions, Keeper," Domina scolds. "We were ancient when you were born and will be guarding the truth long after you are gone."

Bruxa Mala stares daggers at the small dog, but falls silent, aware that despite their small size, these particular dogs are extremely powerful.

"Now, to the matters at hand," Anatra says.

"Cereza, Essence of Dark, Bruxa Mala, Keeper of the Dark, and Charlotte Patisserie, Guardian of the Dark, you have won the last heart in Bakerstown. The fate of all is now in your hands," Anatra says formally.

Lila continues, "You have earned the right to cast the world into Darkness, if that is your wish."

"It is!" Cereza shouts.

"As the victors of the Tipping, that is your choice, though we caution you to move carefully and take great heed of your actions," Anatra warns.

"Yes, yes, whatever," Bruxa Mala dismisses the Dog's warning. "How do we do it?"

Domina explains, "We will guide you to a cave high atop Mount Jadu where near-perfect darkness is held at bay by a single candle. As long as the flame of that candle shines, there will be light in the world. Snuff out the flame, and there will be nothing to stop the Darkness from falling on all."

"That's it?" Mlle. Patisserie says, finally, after mustering enough bravery to speak. "All this work to blow out some stupid candle."

Cereza casts a dirty look at Mlle. Patisserie for her insolent comment, but says in agreement, "All we need to do is blow out the candle, and the Dark wins? Seems easy enough."

"True, snuffing the flame is simple, but living in a world with no light will be far more difficult," Lila explains.

"Enough of this! Take us to the cave." Bruxa Mala demands.

"Very well. Follow us," Anatra says as the three dogs turn and head into the moonless night.

Cereza, Bruxa Mala, Lana, Mlle. Patisserie and Jordi walk toward the door. Anatra steps in front of Lana and Bruxa Mala.

"Not you two. You cannot follow. You must watch from your castle. The final choice to extinguish the flame must be that of the Essence and the Guardian, alone. You cannot interfere."

Knowing she has no choice, Bruxa Mala gives the angriest look ever at the small dog, snaps her fingers and she and her apprentice disappear into blackness.

A voice reaches out from the shadows, "I will be watching," Bruxa Mala cautions, malice dripping from each word. Domina growls deeply, warning the Keeper of the Dark to intrude no further. There's no answer from the shadow. Satisfied the Keeper of the Dark has returned to Castle Dois, the dogs set out for the Cave with the remaining members of the group, Cereza, Mlle. Patisserie and Jordi, following close behind.

Edgar and Toulouse share a quick, worried look before Toulouse runs to catch up. Edgar flies away in the opposite direction.

• • • • •

You see, unlike Mlle. Patisserie, Bruxa Mala and Cereza, Edgar and Toulouse aren't completely bad. As a matter of fact, they're actually quite friendly once you get the know them. They just found themselves in a bad situation.

Years ago, Mlle. Patisserie adopted them when they were just a small kitten and raven chick. She was lonely and they needed a home. It was good fit. At first, life was nice for the three of them. But, as Mlle. Patisserie got more and more bitter toward Ms. Pennybottom, Edgar and Toulouse stopped being pets and turned into the minions we've seen throughout this story.

Life got harder for the cat and raven as Mlle. Patisserie grew darker and meaner. But, at least they were mostly safe, warm and well fed.

When this whole thing with Bruxa Mala and Lana started, Edgar and Toulouse figured it was just another of Mlle. Patisserie's schemes to beat Ms. Pennybottom in the baking competition. As far as they were concerned, that was fine. But, when the Tipping started and Cereza appeared, they began to have doubts about the side they were on.

Both Toulouse and Edgar feel terribly guilty about what happened to Napoleon. Yeah, they think the mouse can be rather annoying, but he didn't deserve what happened. Now, after learning what Cereza and Bruxa Mala have in mind for the entire world, the black cat and raven know they have to do something to stop them.

· · · · ·

"By now, I'm sure the Dogs of Truth are telling Cereza and them how to get rid of the Light forever," Rosie says sadly.

"If only we knew where they were going," Ms. Pennybottom adds. "Maybe we'd have a chance to make everything right."

Tap-tap-tap.

Startled, Ms. Pennybottom looks around to find where the noise is coming from.

Tap-tap-tap.

"Rosie, you hear that?" She asks.

Tap-tap tap.

"I think it's coming from the kitchen," Rosie asserts as she heads out of where they'd been sitting in the living room, trying to figure out a next move. She spots Edgar tapping on the kitchen window with his beak — the same window that just a few hours ago crashed onto their friend.

"You! What do you want?" Rosie throws open the window and asks angrily... well, not so much angrily than in frustration and sadness.

Edgar gestures with his beak, pointing toward the mountain above the town.

"I think he wants us to follow him," Rosie says.

"Why should we trust him? It's his fault Napoleon might not make it," Ms. Pennybottom says, fighting back tears for her furry friend.

Edgar looks down, ashamed.

"Caw. Caaaw. Caaaaaaw," he says, which means "I'm so sorry. I didn't want anyone to get hurt." in Raven-speak.

"I think he really is sorry," she says. "Maybe he knows where Bruxa and Cereza are going," Rosie adds hopefully.

At this statement, Edgar perks up and flaps his wings excitedly.

"I think we should follow him. What do we have to lose?" Rosie presses.

Thinking about it for a moment, Ms. Pennybottom agrees, "You're right, Rosie. We have nothing left to lose."

Turning to Edgar, she commands, "Lead the way, Edgar!" Rosie, Ms. Pennybottom and their new feathered ally head out after team Dark.

• • • • •

THE CAVE, MOUNT JADU, THE NIGHT OF THE FIRST DAY AFTER THE TIPPING

"Welcome to the Cave," Anatra declares.

"It is in this very cavern, ten-thousand years ago today, that two sisters, Lux and Scura, first chose the paths of Light and Dark and created the amulet you now wear," Lila continues, pointing at Cereza's pendant with her nose.

"Deep inside you will find the candle they lit all those millennia ago. The light of a single candle can hold back even the deepest darkness. If it is your decision, extinguish the light of that flame, then the Dark may rule." Domina finishes.

• • • • •

Ravens are fast... Like really fast. They can fly over fifty miles per hour. That's way faster than people can run. They also have great eyesight. Those particular bird facts are coming in very handy for Rosie and Ms. Pennybottom.

Cereza and company had only left Mlle. Patisserie's house a few minutes before Rosie and Ms. Pennybottom left to follow Edgar. The bird was able to fly high enough above Cereza's group that no one noticed him. He then flew back down to guide Rosie and Ms. Pennybottom all the way to the Cave.

Rosie and Ms. Pennybottom get to their destination and hide behind some blackberry bushes just in time to hear the Dogs give their instructions.

"We can't let them blow out that candle," Rosie whispers to Ms. Pennybottom.

"What do we do?" Ms. Pennybottom asks, equally quietly.

"Once they enter the cave, we go in after them and try to stop them," Rosie offers.

"Well, that's as good a plan as any." Ms. Pennybottom agrees. "But, what about Toulouse and that horrible red mouse?" She wonders.

Before Rosie can come up with an answer, Edgar flies over and lands on a stone next to Toulouse. The Dogs are instantly aware of the new arrival but do nothing. The life-long friends share a knowing look. Toulouse glances toward where Rosie and Ms. Pennybottom are hiding and winks.

"I guess that means the cat is on our side, too," Rosie muses.

· · · · ·

Without a word, Cereza and Mlle. Patisserie take their first steps into the Cave to fulfill their destiny.

Toulouse and Jordi wait outside. The Three Dogs of Truth stand guard at the mouth of the cave.

· · · ·

"Okay! Let's go!" Rosie breathes, quietly but excitedly.

She and Ms. Pennybottom set off quickly to follow their Dark rivals into the cavern.

It only takes an instant for Jordi to see Rosie hurrying toward the Cave. Just as she turns to warn Cereza and Mlle. Patisserie, a paw slams down onto her tail. Anatra presses down on her back, pinning her to the ground.

While she was momentarily distracted by the Essence and Guardian of Light coming out of nowhere, Toulouse was able to slink to her side and trap her.

The Three Dogs of Truth glance over at the cat and mouse, amused at the turn of events. They then turn their attention to Rosie and Ms. Pennybottom who are about to pass the threshold of the Cave.

"We were hoping you would find your way here," Domina confesses.

"We were bound to guide whoever won the Tipping, but that does not mean we must bar the other side from entering," Anatra says.

"Good luck, Rosie Petunia!" Lila wishes.

"Thank you," Rosie says, and she and Ms. Pennybottom plunge into the darkness of the cavern.

• • • • •

Lit by the glow of her amulet, Cereza and Mlle. Patisserie explore deeper and deeper into the Cave.

"This cave is huge," Cereza complains. "Where the heck is this candle?"

"It's in here somewhere," Mlle. Patisserie assures. "We just need to keep going."

A few minutes later, the two turn a corner and see a flickering in the distance.

"There it is!" Cereza shouts and sets off at a run toward it. Not wanting to be left alone in the dark, Mlle. Patisserie chases after her and the red light she has around her neck.

• • • • •

Lit by her own glowing pendant, Rosie and Ms. Pennybottom cautiously work their way toward the depths of the Cave, moving carefully not to alert their rivals of their presence.

After what feels like an eternity but is actually only a few tense minutes, the sound of Cereza's shout echoes throughout the cave.

"Oh no! They've found the candle!" Ms. Pennybottom mouths almost silently.

"We need to hurry!" Rosie urges.

Searching through the darkness, they peer further into the Cave and can see the glimmer from Cereza's necklace in the distance. Beyond that is a tiny flickering orange flame.

Both of them quicken their pace, following the beacon that marks the end of their journey.

•••••

The Essence of Dark and her guardian approach a stone ledge where a single candle has stood for ten thousand years. The small flame casts a warm light.

"We've found the Candle!" Cereza says proudly. "This is it!"

Suddenly nervous at the prospect of a world entirely covered in darkness, Mlle. Patisserie pauses. Considering her options, she figures it's better to be on the winning team, darkness or no darkness and says to Cereza, "What are you going to do?"

The young girl answers solemnly, "I was born to do one thing — smother this light and turn the whole world to the Dark. I will fulfill my destiny."

With that Cereza steps forward.

• • • • •

Rosie and Ms. Pennybottom are mere feet from the candle. In the dim light they see Cereza take a deep breath.

"Cereza! Stop!" Rosie shouts. "You don't have to do this!"

Shocked at seeing her opposite, Cereza pauses. She looks straight into the Rosie's eyes and says, simply, "Yes, I do."

Without wasting another second, she blows out the candle.

• • • • •

Outside the Cave, a terrible peal of thunder booms. What was a moonless night is now as dark as onyx as, one-by-one, the stars flicker out. Edgar and Toulouse huddle together, scared, but taking some solace in being together. Jordi is forgotten by the cat and sprints away into the forest, realizing there's nothing left for her to do. The Three Dogs of Truth howl at the sky, mourning at the death of the Light.

• • • • •

BAKERSTOWN, THE FIRST MOMENTS OF THE REIGN OF DARKNESS

A night like no other before it blankets the village of Bakerstown. Even though they're not aware of what happened high above them on Mount Jadu, the people of the town know something has happened...that the world feels different, feels wrong. Front doors open across town as people step outside and stare up at the completely moonless and starless sky. Words of reassurance can be heard up and down the streets as the hopeful promise the fearful that everything will be alright.

• • • • •

CASTLE DOIS, THE FIRST MOMENTS OF THE REIGN OF DARKNESS

Juniper and Bruxa Mala sit at their golden table watching the events at the Cave unfold through the giant crystal ball, in much the same way as they did when this whole ordeal began.

Bruxa Mala is dressed in the finest blood-red gown, her jet-black hair flowing richly over her shoulders. Her violet eyes shine with equal parts triumph and cruelty. She is the most powerful person in the world.

Across from her, Juniper is now even more her sister's opposite. Weakened by the extinguishing of the Light, she can barely lift her head. Her platinum white hair is dull and waxy. Her once bright sky-blue eyes are blurry and dim.

"Well, sister," Juniper manages to speak, weakly. "You've taken my power and the world is yours to do with what you wish. I hope you're happy."

"Happy?" Bruxa squeals. "Happy? I'm ecstatic. For over a thousand years, this is all I've ever wanted. Finally, I've proven that I'm better than you... I've beaten you, and it feels wonderful!"

13

Light Is a Funny Thing...

THE CAVE, MOUNT JADU, THE FIRST MOMENTS OF THE REIGN OF DARKNESS

"You lost! Ha! You're weak and you lost!" Cereza taunts Rosie.

"First I beat you at the bake-off. Then I stole your customers. Now I've destroyed everything you stand for! Admit it, Abby, I'm better than you!" Mlle. Patisserie adds, sneering at Ms. Pennybottom.

Rosie Petunia and Abigail Pennybottom ignore their jeers. They focus on each other.

"It'll be okay, Rosie. We'll find a way to fix this," Ms. Pennybottom promises.

"I know," Rosie replies. "As long as we work together, we have hope."

"Exactly," Ms. Pennybottom says. "You, Napoleon and I, we're a family."

Ms. Pennybottom grabs Rosie and hugs her tightly. "I love you," she whispers.

Rosie realizes for the first time that they really are a family. Ms. Pennybottom is more than just her Guardian; she's her mom. Rosie hugs her back just as tightly. "I love you, too... Mom," Rosie whispers back.

Ms. Pennybottom's heart jumps with happiness in her chest. Despite all the darkness around them, in that hug, Rosie and Ms. Pennybottom don't feel despair and defeat. They feel joy that they have each other. They feel hope.

Slowly, a small white light begins to glimmer, pushing away the darkness. It's not coming from

Rosie's heart-shaped amulet or from the Candle. It's coming from inside Rosie. Brighter and brighter it gets, until, all of a sudden, a beam of light shines out from the middle of her chest. The pure light fills the entire Cave, casting away every single shadow.

"What's happening?" Mlle. Patisserie asks, stricken back by the unexpected blaze.

"It's Rosie!" Ms. Pennybottom answers. "She's... She's glowing!"

All of Rosie is glowing now. Her light is so intense that it's all anyone can see. It shines out beyond the cave, reigniting all of the night sky. For an instant, night becomes day.

After a few moments, the glare dims to a small ember right above Rosie's heart. Mlle. Patisserie and Cereza stare at Rosie, dumbfounded at what just happened.

Ms. Pennybottom rushes to Rosie. "Are you okay?" she asks.

"I'm fine." Rosie responds. "Actually, I'm great!"

From the other side of the cave, Mlle. Patisserie shouts, "Cereza! Your pendant! It's back to the way it was!"

"No! It can't be!" Cereza snarls.

Rosie looks down at her own pendant, which just a few minutes before was radiating blood red. But, now, just like Cereza's it's back to the balance of half diamond and half onyx.

The group all looked over to the Candle, expecting it to be alight once more. It wasn't. The wick was unchanged from when Cereza blew it out.

"No!" Cereza screams again as she picks up the Candle and throws it at Rosie.

"Complain all you like, Cereza, it is no use," a voice says from behind them. It came from Domina. The Three Dogs of Truth stood together in the quivering light.

"Rosie has become one with the Light," Domina says, slightly in awe herself.

"Long ago, the Candle was lit by the first Keepers to give them light on a rainy night. But, light is a funny thing. It can shine out from so many different places, not just candles," Lila explains.

"Tonight, drawn by her love and hope, the Light found a new home in Rosie. She is no longer the Essence of Light, she is the first Light Bearer. As long Rosie lives and as long as hope and love exist in this world, the flame shall endure until she passes it to the next," Lila continues. "Candle or no Candle."

Anatra looks at Rosie and Ms. Pennybottom and says, "You never gave up, even when all seemed lost. Well done."

Then, in a quiet voice meant only for Ms. Pennybottom, Anatra whispers, "Protect her. Without her, the world can still be lost."

"I will," Ms. Pennybottom whispers back. "I promise."

In her relief and happiness Rosie can't resist it any longer. She reaches down and scratches Anatra behind the ears. She is an adorable pup, after all. Her tail wags joyfully. Not wanting to miss out on some quality snuggles, Lila flops down on her back and asks for belly rubs. Ms. Pennybottom has no choice but to do as asked. Domina sighs and thinks,

"Oh, what the heck," and nuzzles under Rosie free hand.

Angry at their defeat and annoyed at those stupid dogs, Cereza and Mlle. Patisserie storm out of the Cave, arguing the whole way home over whose fault it was.

Epilogue

Who's Up for Cake?

BAKERSTOWN, THE FIRST DAY OF THE NEW BALANCE

With a miniscule cast on his little paw, Napoleon limps across the kitchen counter toward a very enticing piece of chocolate lava cake. Having traded in his tiny sword for an equally tiny pair of crutches, it takes him a while to get there. A new addition to the Pennybottom household, Toulouse, pushes the cake closer to the injured mouse.

"At least he still has his appetite," Rosie jokes as she tears a piece of bread off the French dip sandwich she's eating and tosses it to the other new addition, Edgar. He snatches it out of the air happily.

"Thank goodness for small miracles," Ms. Pennybottom laughs. She looks around at her new family and smiles.

On their way back home from the Cave, Rosie and Ms. Pennybottom stopped at the vet to check on Napoleon, fearing the worst. Thankfully, Dr. Dyr was able to save the Lilliputian fella.

"He'll have to wear a cast for a little while, but he should make a full recovery," he told Ms. Pennybottom when he brought Napoleon back home earlier that morning.

Ms. Pennybottom and Rosie could not be more grateful. They're so grateful, in fact, they're baking him the biggest lemon-raspberry cake ever.

This day is almost perfect, but Ms. Pennybottom realizes it's missing one important thing, or rather one important person, Hector Pantalones. She's been trying to reach him all morning. She even knocked on his door to share the amazing events. No answer. As a matter of fact, no one has seen him since the day before.

Making a mental note to try again later, Ms. Pennybottom says to everyone, "Okay, who's up for cake?"

• • • • •

CASTLE DOIS, THE FIRST DAY OF THE NEW BALANCE

Bruxa Mala slams her fists on the table hard enough to rattle the huge crystal ball.

"I can't believe it!" she screams. "We'd won! This isn't possible! It can't be over!"

With the balance restored, Juniper is feeling more herself. She says, "My sister, it appears some lights can never be smothered."

"I had a good feeling about Abigail," she adds, smiling, looking down at her own pendant.

Nata joins the pair at the table and says, "You have to see this," as she sets down the Book of Balance.

"Look," she points out, "The empty pages...They're full of writing. Everything about this story is there. Rosie, Cereza, everything!"

Bruxa Mala and Juniper leaf through the pages, reading the tale of the past several days. On the last page, both Keepers' eyes grow wide.

"See, my dear Juniper, I knew this wasn't over," Bruxa Mala says, malevolently.

A look of worry creeps back onto Juniper's face.

THE END.

The First Review of
The Misadventures of Rosie Petunia

Dear Nick,

I LOVED! The Misadventures Of Rosie Petunia! I couldn't stop reading it, Also the book was soooo good I couldn't stop reading it I read it in only something around 3 hours!

I have a few suggestions.

One, I think one word was incorrect, On page 66 you wrote ten-hour old person, did you mean 10 year old person?

My last suggestion which is more like a question is are you making another part, I hope you are! My favorite character is Rosie because she's so sweet litterally. In conclusion, I think it should be a book that should sell instore and the age range I think should range from 7-10. I LOVED the book thank you for giving me an early look at it!!! Sincerely, Sienna

– Sienna Boccio

ABOUT THE AUTHORS

Hi. We're Nick and Cristina Glasnovich. *The Misadventures of Rosie Petunia* is the first book we've written together.

Nick works in digital communications and is a designer. He's a big fan of superheroes, cooking, cars, watches and the Green Bay Packers.

Cristina works in the luxury goods industry. She loves music, fantasy books, animals (especially dogs and horses) and has a pretty great imagination.

We came up with the character of Rosie Petunia one night, and it only took seven years for *The Misadventures of Rosie Petunia* to finally become a book.

Just a bit of trivia...We named "The Three Dogs of Truth" after our three real dogs, Domino, Ducky and Lily.

Made in the USA
Middletown, DE
17 June 2021